BITTEN AT DAYBREAK

Last Witch Standing, Book 3

DEANNA CHASE

Bayou Moon Publishing

Copyright © 2019 by Deanna Chase

First Edition 2019

Cover Art by Ravven

Edited by Anne Victory and Angie Ramey

ISBN 978-1-940299-76-1

Bayou Moon Publishing

About This Book

Badass witch Phoebe Kilsen has spent years looking for her brother. Now that she's found him, her world is turned upside down and everything she has ever known to be true appears to be false. Cut off from everyone except her brother, can she find a way back to her partner Dax, her best friend Willow, and her life's work with the Void? Or will she be destined to live a lie with a vampire she's never trusted?

Chapter One

*E*adric Allcot dropped his hand under the table and placed it on my thigh. My fingers twitched, aching for my dagger, the one I usually carried strapped to my ankle. The one that was lying on my dresser in my new alternate-reality dressing room. It didn't exactly go with my respectable dress and the boring high heels I'd been expected to wear.

He was lucky I didn't have my weapon, otherwise the dagger would've been lodged in his groin. Tightening my jaw, I grabbed his hand and placed it back in his own lap. The vampire, whom I'd been told was my husband less than thirty minutes ago, cast me a confused look but kept his hand to himself.

I glanced over at my brother. His dark head was bent close to Pandora's blond one as they whispered something to each other. The contented smile that passed over Seth's face made my stomach churn with anxiety. In the world I lived in, Pandora was Allcot's consort, not my brother's wife. And the pair were a thousand percent committed to each other. The

Allcot I knew would've ripped Seth's heart out just for looking at his woman like that.

But we weren't in my world. Earlier today, I'd accidentally slipped through the fabric of the universe and ended up in an alternate reality. And then gotten stuck here when my doppelgänger realized what had happened before I did and took my place in my world, effectively closing the temporarily open window. There was no going back. At least not yet.

The only person who knew I wasn't the Phoebe Kilsen of this world was my brother Seth. He assured me that confessing my true identity would likely get me killed. If Allcot knew his real wife was gone and it was my fault, all hell would break loose. So for now I was trapped in some alternate universe where nothing made sense to me and only one person knew my true identity. How could I, in any form of myself, have ended up married to a vampire? I was a vampire hunter, for fuck's sake.

"Phoebe can spell the ring," Allcot said to his associate.

"What ring? And why?" I asked, shaken out of my thoughts.

The dark-skinned vampire sitting across the table gave me a patient, almost condescending smile as he tapped the large sapphire stone on his right ring finger. "Death spell. Can't walk into Clio La Doux's without a few tricks up my sleeve, now can I?"

Death spell. Christ. What had I gotten myself into? I definitely could cast such a curse. But I sure as hell didn't want to. That was some serious shit. "Why do you need it for Clio La Doux's place?"

Everyone—the four vamps who were there on Allcot's orders as well as my brother, his wife, and Allcot himself—turned to stare at me.

Allcot's brow furrowed. His gaze searched mine as if he was trying to understand something. "Is everything all right, Phoebs?"

Phoebs. That's what my best friend Willow called me. My stomach churned with unease. Would I ever see her again? Was she here in this world? And if she was, did she run a magical bakery in Uptown New Orleans?

"She's fine," Seth said. "Just a little depleted. We worked on some potions today. Healing potions to combat those poisonous darts La Doux's team surprised us with last time."

I turned my attention to him and mouthed, *Poisonous darts?*

He gave me a tiny shake of his head, indicating we weren't talking about it now.

Dammit. I hated being lost. But I wasn't prepared to tell anyone I wasn't the Phoebe they thought I was. Only Seth knew, and I was going to keep it that way. I had no idea what Allcot would do with that information. If this Allcot was anything like the one I knew, he'd find a way to manipulate me.

"Like Seth said, we were busy with those potions." I gave Allcot a fake sheepish smile. "My brain might need a rest."

"That's okay, gorgeous," Allcot said, his voice full of tenderness. "We'll get you to bed early tonight." My husband, the vampire Eadric Allcot, slipped his hand back to my knee, just under the hem of my skirt, and slid his fingers up my thigh, thankfully stopping before he reached the promised land.

I gritted my teeth and prayed for his sake he didn't move his hand higher. My self-control was a little perilous, and I was afraid I'd neuter him with my butter knife. No wonder he'd wanted me to wear the Betty Crocker blue-and-white polka-dot dress instead of my torn jeans and kick-ass boots. Easy access to grope me under the table while he talked business with his lackey vampires.

"Okay, Phoebe spells the ring; I'll have my associate set the tracker," the dark-skinned vamp said. He ran his hand over his bald head. "Let's just hope Genevieve got the message."

All the vampires turned to look at me again. I started to sweat. Obviously I'd been in charge of the message, and I had no idea what to say. "I—"

"Genevieve got the message. Don't worry, the back door will be open and the security cameras disabled," Seth said with a decisive nod. "Phoebe got a text about an hour ago."

"Good." Allcot let out a breath he didn't need to hold and caressed my thigh with his thumb. "Then we're all set for tomorrow." He flicked his icy gray gaze at the vampire in front of me. "Leave the ring with Phoebe, Sterling. She can take care of it in the morning when she casts the illusion spells for us."

Every nerve ending screamed for me to break Allcot's fingers, but I held it together thanks to the filet mignon on my plate. It was the most tender piece of beef I'd ever had the pleasure of wrapping my lips around. I chewed on the meat and scanned the guests. Besides Sterling, there were three other vampires. One was downright gorgeous. George Clooney gorgeous with his dark hair, inky black eyes, and sun-kissed skin. The one to his right sported bleached-blond hair, pale blue eyes, three eyebrow piercings, and a trail of thorns tattooed on his neck. I decided he looked like Spike. And the fourth one had very pale skin, an average build, and intelligent green eyes that seemed to track everyone at all times. He was paying particular attention to me, studying me and frowning as if he was troubled by something. I nearly chuckled. He should be. If any of them got out of line or handsy, I wouldn't hesitate to stake them.

"Hey, Kai," Seth said from the other end of the table.

The medium-built vampire twisted and glanced at Seth. "What is it?"

"Can you write up a detail on everything we know about Clio and her operation? I want to study it to see if there's any connections or vulnerabilities we're missing."

Allcot let out an amused laugh. "Kilsen, you're such an old lady. This isn't a classroom. No one needs a book report."

"Humor me," Seth said to the vampire he called Kai.

Kai narrowed his eyes at my brother and then gave him a short nod. "Sure, boss. I'll have it to you later tonight."

Allcot picked up his wineglass and lifted it high for a toast. "To the end of Clio's reign."

Everyone, including Pandora who'd been silent through the exchange, lifted their glass. Allcot glanced at me, then my untouched wineglass, and back to me as his grip tightened on my thigh. The irritation on his face was unmistakable.

I swallowed a sigh and lifted the glass. "To the end of Clio's reign," I said, having no idea who Clio was or why she needed to be taken down.

When the dinner was over, I immediately started helping Pandora clear the table and was completely annoyed by the fact that none of the men helped or even acknowledged our effort. They just moved as a group to Allcot's study, leaving the women to do the domestic work. Fuming, probably more from being stuck in an alternate reality than because I was doing dishes, I dropped a stack of plates on the counter and stalked back into the dining room for another load of bullshit. I returned with my hands full of wineglasses.

Pandora took them from me and gently put them in the sink.

"I could've done that," I said.

"Oh no. Not with that bee up your ass. These are my great-grandmother's, and if they had gotten the dish treatment, we were going to have words." Her tone was no-nonsense, but her eyes glinted with amusement.

"Bee up my ass?" I asked, raising one eyebrow as I stared at the gorgeous blonde.

"Yeah. What's up with that? You were so tense when Eadric was touching you that I thought you were going claw his eyes out. Trouble in paradise?"

So she'd noticed. Probably everyone had. Subtle wasn't usually my strong suit. "Just not in the mood, I guess."

"That's a first," she said almost to herself and went back to washing the dishes.

Good goddess. Did that mean what I thought it meant? Was Allcot going to expect me to serve myself up on a silver platter after his vamps left? I closed my eyes and said a silent prayer. I needed to get out of there. Back to my own world. But Seth had already said that I couldn't share time with my doppelgänger, and the only way I was going to get back was if she came here first. I didn't understand why it couldn't work the other way around. But I sure as hell was going to find out.

"Hey, Phoebe," Pandora said, placing a plate into the commercial-grade dishwasher. The kitchen was outfitted with high-end appliances and was big enough that it likely could handle service for a small restaurant.

"Yeah?" I finished stuffing leftovers into the refrigerator.

"Can you work on a protection spell for Seth? Yours are so much better than his, and I know he won't ask. But when you guys storm the castle tomorrow, I want him to be protected by your ancient family magic."

"Of course." There was nothing to think about. Seth was the only family I had in this world, and protecting him was a no-brainer. But I also needed information. Treading carefully, I asked, "Do you think it's going to be a bloodbath tomorrow?"

"Definitely. Clio isn't going to be happy when her girls go missing. Even if you guys do manage to sneak them out, she'll retaliate. We'll need to be ready."

Girls? Missing? Was Allcot into trafficking? Bile rose up in the back of my throat. No. It wasn't possible. Seth would never be involved in something like that. Not the Seth I knew anyway. And he definitely was the man I'd grown up with. There was no question about that. He'd been missing for the past eight years, and when I'd accidently crossed over, I'd found out why. He'd been here, married to a human Pandora. But he hadn't changed, and under no circumstances could I imagine him engaging in trafficking.

"Phoebe?" Pandora asked.

"Huh?" I glanced up into her bright blue eyes.

"What's wrong?" She placed her elegant hand on my arm and squeezed slightly. It was a warmth she'd never possessed in her vampire form. It must be her humanity. "You seem… worried or stressed."

"Just the night-before-the-hunt jitters I guess," I said with a shrug and a half smile. More like get-me-the-fuck-out-of-here nerves, but that was a secret between me and Seth. Would he tell her? I had no idea what kind of marriage they had.

"Sure. That makes sense." She said the words, but her brow was furrowed and she was frowning. It didn't take a genius to know she didn't believe me. But what else was she going to say?

"Mommy, mommy!" A little boy with brown hair and eyes exactly like Pandora's ran into the kitchen, waving a book. He was wearing cotton pajamas with bright red crawfish all over them. "It's story time."

She wrapped her arms around the lanky kid, pulled him up into a hug, and spun around. "My favorite part of the day," she said and nuzzled his cheek with her nose. "What are we reading tonight?"

A huge grin split his lips. "*How Jackson Tamed the Dragon.*"

"Again?" Pandora said with a laugh.

"Again!"

"Okay, dove. Let's go curl up on your bed." She took him by the hand, smiled at me, and followed her child out of the kitchen.

I poked my head into the hall of the big plantation house, heard the low murmurs from the men coming from a room off to the left, and glanced around at the fancy formal living room and then the TV room in the back of the house. And when there was nothing left to explore on the bottom floor, I took a deep breath and headed upstairs to the room I shared with Allcot. I'd been in it once before, when I'd changed into the blue-and-white polka-dot dress, but I hadn't had time to take it in or even process anything. Now I did.

The big canopy bed sat in the middle of the room, the red silk bedspread so predicable that I actually laughed. The Allcot I knew in my world also had a thing for red. But the thought of sharing the bed with him sent a chill down my spine. I was supposed to be with Dax, my shifter partner, the only man I'd ever really let myself love.

The image of him floated in my mind and tears stung

the backs of my eyes. Was he with the other Phoebe? Probably not. If she had managed to make it back to my place, it would be no problem for her to send him away since Dax and I didn't live together. I winced at the thought. Would Dax know she was an imposter? Hope blossomed deep in my chest. He had to know. Dax *knew* me. He'd figure it out. I held on to that hope and went into the adjoining room.

I'd been expecting a sitting room, or another office for Allcot, but instead I found herbs, silver daggers, and a whole collection of agates. I ran my fingers over them, feeling familiar magic contained within the items, and as crazy as it was, I breathed a sigh of relief. If my doppelgänger had spelled these, then our power was the same in both worlds. At least I still had that. Seth and my magic. It was a start.

The sun started to set, and I let myself get lost in a spell text. It wasn't something I'd ever seen before, and more than likely it didn't even exist in my world. If it did, surely I'd have heard of it. The spells were exquisite, inspired even, and I admired the witch's technique. I sat at the worktable and was halfway through the book when suddenly something cool pressed over my pulse in my neck.

I flinched, more from the shock of finding Allcot just behind me. I hadn't even heard him come in.

"Like that, baby?" he asked, pressing his cool lips to my pulse.

"No," I said automatically and jerked away from his too-close fangs.

He stood and moved in close, not respecting my personal space. "No? Since when?"

Dammit. I sucked in a breath, trying to keep my cool. Then I placed my hand on his chest and gave him a gentle push back. "I was busy working on something. I'd like to get back to it."

He stared me in the eye, his steely gray gaze pinning me where I stood. "You weren't yourself at dinner either."

It was a statement, not a question. I didn't bother to answer. Eadric Allcot was just going to have to learn to respect women. I'd make sure of it.

"Are you saying you want to sleep alone tonight, Phoebe?" he asked, surprising me.

"Yes. To get my rest before tomorrow."

He nodded as if my statement was perfectly normal and moved in close, invading my personal space again. Then he tipped my head up so that I was looking into his ridiculously handsome face.

"Allcot, I'm not—"

His eyes flashed with unmistakable suspicion, and before I could even form another thought, he grabbed my arm, spun me so that my back was to his chest, and then held me there as he whispered, "You're not Phoebe."

"Yes I am. Allcot, what—"

"Phoebe never calls me Allcot," he growled.

Shit on a stick. I'd fucked that up royally. How had I been so off my game? I was a highly trained agent of the Void. All it took was one trip to an alternate-universe and it was as if I had zero concept of being undercover. Of course a wife wouldn't call her husband by his last name. She probably even had a pet name for him that no one else would know.

His hold tightened around my waist, and one thumb fluttered over my rapidly beating pulse. "You look like her. Hell, you even smell like her. But do you *taste* like her?"

I stiffened, panic hitting me hard. He was too strong. I'd never break his hold, but if I had a spell... I reached for the necklace I always wore around my neck, the one that would knock out even the oldest of vampires, but my hand only clasped air. The necklace was gone.

"Eadric." I tried one more time. "You're being paranoid. It's just been a strange night. I'm—"

"There's only one way to find out," he said, and then without warning, I felt the sharp sting of a vampire bite.

"Allcot, you fucking bastard!" I screamed, clawing at his arm clutching me. "Stop it. I didn't give you permission to bite me. Stop!" I kicked my foot back, praying I'd connect with his balls, but instead I just got his thigh.

He shifted his weight to the other side and started to suck. As my blood spilled into his mouth, euphoria took over and a sensation so sweet, so glorious, overtook me, making me sigh with pure pleasure. I couldn't help it. I gave in and sagged against him as I let out a small whimper.

Gods, I thought. *Don't ever let it stop.*

Chapter Two

*A*llcot tore his teeth from me, picked me up, and threw me so hard I slammed against the wall in my studio. My head hit the plaster with a loud thunk, dazing me as I slid to the ground and crumpled before him.

"Fucking bitch," he snarled. "Whose blood have you been drinking?"

My head spun, and nausea took over. I'd just gotten out of the infirmary and I had a strong suspicion that by the time he was done, I was going to be in desperate need of another healer. I placed both hands on my head, trying to stop the spinning. "What?" I asked, confused. "I don't drink blood."

"Don't fucking lie to me." He walked up to me, his pointed leather boots showing signs of wear, something I'd never see in my own universe. Allcot was always impeccably dressed from head to toe no matter if he was wearing a suit or just a silk robe. "It's faint, but I can taste it on my tongue. Since when does my *wife* drink from other vamps?"

Horror filled me as a realization dawned. He was

implying that my doppelgänger drank his blood. A vamp's blood. But why?

Power. I'd heard vampire blood could be used for certain dark spells, spells I'd never consider wielding. Not to mention the idea of drinking vampire blood repulsed me.

I needed to fix this and fast. It was just my luck that I'd had a blood transfusion recently. That damned gun wound was still causing me issues. Remembering my brother had told me that Allcot thought we were trying for kids, I took a shot in the dark and said, "It's not another vamp's blood. It's some herbs to help with… fertility."

Allcot, who looked like he'd been ready to tear my head off, blinked in surprise and then took a step back. "Herbs? What kind?"

Having no idea what exactly he'd tasted, I didn't get into the specific herbs that could increase fertility. Instead, I said, "It was a combination I got in New Orleans. I'm not sure exactly what was in it. The healer said it would help."

The anger vanished, and for the first time in my life, I actually saw regret flash over his features. "Shit, Phoebe. God. I'm sorry." He knelt and pressed a palm to my cheek. "You're all right, aren't you? Do you need ice? Fuck. I handled that all wrong."

"You think?" I snapped and pushed myself to my feet. Stomping past my abuser, I decided I couldn't blame my doppelgänger for taking my spot in my world. If that was what this version of Allcot was like, I would've jumped realities too. Fuck. That meant she wasn't coming back. I was going to have to talk my brother into going after her and forcing her back.

I'd just learned that my brother's doppelgänger in this world had died and that's why he was able to slip in and out of the two worlds without an issue. He chose this one because of his son. I understood it, but I still hadn't come to terms with it.

"Phoebe, please," Allcot said, his voice quiet. "You know how it is with the other vampires in this town. I just get so…"

"Jealous?" I finished for him, letting my contempt show. "Attack me again, and I'll stake you myself."

The words had flown out of my mouth before I could stop and think about what I'd said. But I didn't care. No one attacked me and got away with it. I fully expected him to go into another rage, but instead he just chuckled.

"I always knew marrying you would be an adventure. You never disappoint." He walked over to me, his eyes blazing with lust.

My stomach turned. What the hell did he think he was doing? He'd just slammed me against the wall. This wasn't some BDSM fantasy.

He dipped his head down, going in for a kiss as his arm came around my waist.

But I placed my hand on his chest and gave him a good shove. "I don't think so, buddy. You don't get to toss me around the room and then rip my clothes off. The baby-making plans are postponed."

His lips twitched as if he found me funny. "For how long?"

"Indefinitely." I glared at him, but my ire only seemed to fuel his amusement.

He stepped in close again and grinned. "So. You're going to make me work for it then?"

I wanted to slap the cocky grin right off his face. My anger wasn't fake, and right about then I was feeling a collective rage on behalf of women everywhere. The sick bastard actually thought he had a chance of getting into my pants after he went psycho on me. No. No way. Not ever. It was obvious this wasn't the first time he'd lost his temper, and it made me wonder how the other Phoebe handled it. Did she put him in his place? Go along with his bullshit just because it was easier? If it was the latter, I sincerely hoped she'd been planning his demise carefully.

"You're going to take a step back and let me decide when and if I want you in my bed," I said, my tone so cold it could've frozen his dick right off.

His piercing blue eyes narrowed and his irritation flashed. "Fine. Then stay the fuck out of my room. You can sleep here in your studio. But hear me on this. No one in this house is going to know you've denied me, got that?"

"Fine." I matched his glare with one of my own. "But if you lay a hand on me again, what they think of our sex life is going to be the least of your worries."

We were both silent. He stared at me as if really looking at me for the first time. I started to wonder if he was questioning my true identity again. But then he reached out, squeezed my hand and said, "It won't happen again. My apologies, love."

Love. I wanted to vomit as I watched him turn on his heel and stride out, his head held high.

I let out a long breath and clutched the desk as my hands started to shake. He couldn't be trusted. He'd hurt me once, and he'd certainly do it again. Not that I'd give him a chance. That dagger was going to be a permanent accessory from now on, and I wasn't afraid to use it. At least the expectation of sharing his bed had been removed. It was something.

And I didn't have to share his bed. I glanced over at the couch under the window. It would certainly do as long as

Allcot stayed away. I took my time searching through the attached walk-in closet and was relieved to find an extra blanket and a pillow on the top shelf. Knowing that Allcot was likely downstairs, I raided the master bedroom closet and found myself pajamas and a change of clothes and deposited them in my studio.

I was busy logging the spelled jewelry on my worktable when I heard a light knock on the door. My entire body stiffened. If Allcot was back for round two, there'd probably be bloodshed, only this time it would be his.

The second knock was louder.

"Phoebe?" Seth called. "Are you in there?"

The tension drained from my shoulders, and I walked over, flipped the lock, and let him in.

"Jesus fuck, Phoebs." He reached up and gently turned my head to the side. "Did that bastard bite you?"

"I think the evidence speaks for itself," I said, trying to swallow my rage. I needed answers, and Seth was the only one who could give them to me. "Forget it. I'm fine. We… worked it out."

His eyebrows shot up. "What does that mean exactly?"

"It means I threatened to cut his dick off if he ever put his fucking hands or teeth on me again."

Seth's brown eyes turned almost black as he paled. "You didn't."

"Well, not exactly, but that was the gist. He won't be doing that again." I crossed my arms over my chest, leaned against the desk, and nodded to the couch. "We've also come to an agreement. I'll be sleeping here for the foreseeable future."

"Damn, little sis," he said, sounding impressed. "I gotta

say, I had no idea how you were going to handle this. Well done."

I rolled my eyes. "If you thought I was going to sleep with that vampire, you've lost your mind. He's even worse in this reality than he is in ours."

Seth sucked in a deep breath. "I can see why you'd say that, but there are things you need to know. He might not be as bad as you think he is."

"I'm all ears, but you won't change my mind. He is as bad as I think," I insisted, my ire rising to inferno levels. "That bastard threw me against the wall when he thought I'd been drinking another vampire's blood."

"He... what?" Seth's expression turned confused. "You're drinking vampire blood now?"

"Of course not. You know I would never engage in vampire blood magic. Hell, Seth. Do you really think I've changed that much?" I stared at him like he had three heads, and I had a strong desire to punch something. How in the hell had this happened? Dax's face flashed in my mind, and I had to fight back a scream. He was the only person I wanted in that moment, but instead I was stuck with my jackass brother and Eadric fucking Allcot.

"No," Seth said, rubbing his jaw. "I don't think that. I just don't know why your blood would taste different."

"Because of the blood transfusion I just had. If you hadn't just disappeared on me, you'd know those details."

He glanced down at his feet, clearly uncomfortable. "I'm sorry, Phoebe. It's just... Pandora and my boy. I had to get home."

I closed my eyes and took a deep breath, trying for calm. "You know, you could've just told me. If I'd known, I wouldn't have been looking for you and this never would've happened." Son of a… Gah! I was seriously pissed at him, and it took all my willpower to not slug him.

"I didn't tell you precisely because I didn't want you to follow me." A muscle in his jaw pulsed. "This crossing realities, it's dangerous, Phoebe. I was just trying to save you from this happening."

"I'm not a sixteen-year-old anymore, Seth. I can be trusted with information. In fact, I'm pretty damned competent. You'd know that if you paid any attention."

"You're right." He ran a hand through his thick dark hair and moved to sit on the couch. "Look at what you've done with Allcot in less than two hours. If he's not careful, you're going to be running this show soon." He gave me a half smile.

I took a seat next to him, feeling some of my rage fade. "Was that a compliment? I think you just complimented me."

His smile widened to a grin. "Maybe."

His approval filled me up and eased some of the heartache I'd been carrying around for the past eight years.

"Listen," he said as he reached around to his back pocket and pulled out a folded-up envelope. "I know you think Allcot is a bastard. And he probably is, but he's more than that. What we're doing tomorrow is important. Clio's operation is one of the dirtiest. If we're successful, it will mean freeing dozens of women from forced prostitution."

"Clio La Doux is a madam?" I asked, still trying to process his words.

"More than that. She's a predator of the worst kind. She used her magic to coerce these women into contracts, and then they're stuck for decades working for her."

I took the envelope he was still holding and retrieved the packet of papers inside. But before I looked at it, I asked, "Why does Allcot care?"

"Why do you think he wouldn't care, Phoebe?" he asked, sounding annoyed at the question.

"Because, brother, the Allcot I know never does anything unless there's something in it for him."

He shrugged one shoulder. "I'm sure he'd like to take La Doux down. She causes a lot of problems in the city, not just for vampires but the paranormal community in general. She has politicians as well as drug dealers on her payroll, and she deals in everything from adult entertainment to predatory housing. She fleeces the city, manipulates those she can, and eliminates those she can't. But if you ask me, his main reason is you."

"Me?" I jerked back. "Why?"

"Take a look at the list of names. The one at the top."

I scanned the document that the vampire Kai had prepared for Seth, and a cold chill ran down my spine. The name at the top of the list of those Clio had entrapped was none other than my best friend Willow Rhoswen.

Chapter Three

"*M*arrok. Good. You're here," Director Halston said the moment he walked into her office. She glanced past him and barked, "Where's Kilsen? Her healer said she's cleared for work."

Dax stared at the director, not sure what to say. He had no idea. She'd taken a bullet for him and a bunch of other people over a week ago after a shifter had tried to drug and turn Dax and a couple of others into rabid killers using an illegal drug. She'd saved them by sacrificing herself and had just left the infirmary the day before, but she hadn't called him last night nor returned his calls this morning. He cleared his throat. "I haven't heard from her since before she left the infirmary."

Halston, the director of the Void division of the Arcane —the government paranormal investigation agency—blinked at him from her spot behind her desk. "What do you mean you haven't heard from her? I thought you two were... involved."

They were, but that didn't mean they were joined at the

hip. Phoebe was the independent sort. Still, he'd been planning to go over to her place the night before to check in on her but had ended up working late and bringing in a rogue vampire. By the time he'd gotten home, he'd assumed she'd be asleep and had decided to let her rest. He'd figured he'd see her this morning, but so far he hadn't heard one word. "It's not like we live together."

"I see." The short, gray-haired fae grunted. "She's still your partner, no?"

Of course she was. And the director damned well knew it. She was the only one who had the power to change their assignments. "Yes."

"Then I suggest you track her down, because you two have a new case." Her dark eyes flashed with anger as she tossed a folder at him. "There's been an attack. A young shifter was killed in the Garden District."

Dax felt his jaw tighten. The shifters and vampires had been at war for a while in the Crescent City, but with the help of the most powerful vampire in the city, Eadric Allcot, there'd been a tentative agreement for each side to settle down. An attack would end the truce, and Dax would be back to square one. "Any information on which vampire did it? I thought tensions had settled."

"It wasn't a vampire. This one looks like a nasty death spell. There's one pissed-off witch in the city. I need you and Kilsen to find whoever it is and bring them in ASAP. The shifter population is already restless. They won't wait too long to take matters into their own hands."

She was right. The shifters roaming around New Orleans had recently lost their pack leader. And without someone to keep them in line, they'd be burning witches at the stake in no time. "I'm on it. I might enlist Leo to help us out. Is that all right?"

She gave him a short nod. "I don't see why not. He's been doing very well in his classes this past week. He could use some fieldwork."

"Thanks." Dax had taken the young shifter under his wing a few months back. He'd lost his girl to a nasty drug recently and work helped him cope with life. Dax tucked the file under his arm and moved toward the door. "We'll get to work on this right away."

She kept her head down and didn't even acknowledge his comment. Dax strode out without another word and headed straight for the office he shared with Phoebe. He'd been expecting to find his partner or at least signs that she'd been there. Instead, the office was dark and her clean coffee cup was still hanging on the wall above the coffee maker. At least he knew she hadn't visited the office. That mug wouldn't have lasted five minutes on that hook.

He took a seat, tried Phoebe's phone again, but didn't leave a message when all he got was voice mail. She already had enough of those from him. Instead, he sent a text:

Is everything all right? We have a new case. A witch appears to have murdered a shifter. Call me or let me know when you'll be here.

Dax wasn't surprised when she didn't answer. It wasn't like her to miss a meeting with the director. The fact that she hadn't shown meant she was tied up with something. He just hoped he heard from her sooner rather than later. He wasn't a worrier by nature, but she had been shot recently, and it was going on twenty-four hours since he'd heard from her. He trusted Healer Imogen to not release Phoebe unless she was ready, but until he saw his partner in her tight jeans, wielding her dagger, that gnawing in his gut wasn't likely to go away.

After fixing himself a cup of coffee, he sat down at his desk and read over the file. The woman, Maci Masterson, had been twenty-seven years old and came from a prominent shifter family in New Orleans. Her father sat on the city council and was a partner in a prestigious law firm. Her mother was from a wealthy family that made their money in sugarcane, and had gone on to make a name for herself, running a nonprofit for low-income paranormals who landed in the city.

The fact that Maci was killed by a witch was going to be a huge scandal in the city. News reports likely had already started airing, and the papers would be reporting every tiny detail they could scrounge up.

"Great," Dax muttered to himself. Investigating this one was going to be a bitch. The reporters were going to be all up in his business, probably fucking up his progress. He glanced at the details. The woman had been found just after sunrise, her skin ashen and leathery as if she'd aged eight years before taking her last breath. The death curse had certainly done its job.

He shuddered, trying to shake off the visual.

When he scanned the cataloged list of her personal items, he frowned. She'd still been carrying her designer purse. As far as he could tell, nothing had been taken from it. Her wallet, credit cards, cash, and even her eight-hundred-dollar phone were still present. This hadn't been a simple robbery gone bad the way the media would speculate. This had been a full-on attack. And the killer was still out there.

But why? That was the question. What would a witch have to gain by killing the shifter? He didn't know, but it was his job to find out. Pushing back from his desk, he rose from the chair and headed down to the Void's morgue. The fluorescent lights illuminated the stark white halls, and his shoes squeaked on the tile floors. No one was around. The researchers were locked away behind their steel doors while the other agents were out in the city, hunting down leads.

Dax used his ID card to enter the cold room. A tall, thin, dark-skinned witch sat at his desk, rapidly typing. His hair had turned gray, but other than that, he didn't look a day over thirty-five.

"Mateo, you got a minute?"

The paranormal examiner swung his chair around, a tiny smile making his lips twitch. "Marrok. I thought I'd be hearing from you soon. Where's Kilsen?"

"Not sure. She might be taking one more day before she comes back in to work," he guessed. "But we just got a new case and I'm hoping you can get me some information."

"Sure." Mateo rose from the chair, all six foot eight of the guy towering over him. Dax wasn't a short man, measuring over six feet himself.

"I'm here about Maci Masterson. Do you have any details on her death yet?"

Mateo walked over to a table and pulled back a sheet, exposing a corpse.

Dax swallowed the bile in the back of his throat and followed him. The shifter had seen more than his share of death over the years. It was unavoidable when working for the Void, but it wasn't every day that the victim was a young woman who'd had her whole life in front of her.

Blond hair splayed out over the table. There were diamond studs in her ears that had to be at least three carats each. And her expensive-looking lace cocktail dress was unmarred. However she'd died, there hadn't been much of a fight. In fact, there wasn't anything to Dax's eye that indicated a fight at all.

"Do you have any idea what happened?" Dax asked.

"Sure do." Mateo turned the woman's head, exposing her neck to Dax. "See that brand right there?"

Dax squinted at the small burn mark in her neck. "Yeah."

"That was where the spell hit her. If I had to guess, I'd say the witch used a cursed piece of metal, likely a ring, to end this wolf's life. By burning the spell into her skin, she never had a chance. The spell would've hit her blood stream and killed her within twenty minutes."

Unease settled in Dax's gut as he stared at the vine pattern with a small fleur-de-lis right in the center. He'd seen it before. He just wasn't sure where. "And this spell did what? Stop her heart?"

"More or less," the examiner said. "It paralyzed her major organs, causing them to fail. It's the type of spell that only really powerful witches can wield." He glanced down at his notes. "We're running some DNA tests to see if we get any hits, but so far it's not looking good. I didn't find any obvious evidence of a struggle, and that means there might not be anything under her fingernails to test."

"That's not a lot to go on."

"We've given you and your partner less before, and you always seem to manage."

"You're right about that." Dax pulled out his phone and quickly took a picture of the burn mark on the shifter's neck. It actually was an excellent clue. If he could just place where he'd seen it before, he'd be in business. "Thanks, man. Will you let me know if anything comes back from testing?"

"You got it." Mateo covered the girl and then shuffled

back to his desk while Dax headed back to his office. When it was clear Phoebe still hadn't arrived, he grabbed the file and took off. He needed to find his partner.

Dax didn't want to admit it to himself, but he was worried. The events over the past few weeks had left him unsettled. All he wanted was to see Phoebe and make sure she was all right.

Frustrated, he put his car in gear and sped over to the house Phoebe shared with Willow Rhoswen and her husband Talisen. The house was dark, no cars in the driveway. He parked on the street and strolled up to the house. His knock went unanswered. He didn't make a habit of just walking into her house unannounced, but she had given him a key and it was about time he used it.

The Greek Revival townhome was silent except for his footsteps on the old hardwood. The living room was tidy, as was Phoebe's bedroom at the foot of the stairs. Her bed was made, indicating she likely hadn't slept in it. She wasn't one for making her bed every morning. After scanning the downstairs, he headed up to the second story, finding the kitchen empty. After a quick peek into Willow and Talisen's room, it was crystal clear that no one was home, not even Link. He blew out a breath and headed back downstairs.

Dax had just intended to leave Phoebe a note to let her know he'd been there, but as he was searching for a notepad among the stuff on her small desk, a picture caught his eye. It was one of Phoebe and her brother. One he'd seen a dozen times before. But this time instead of admiring his girl's good looks, his attention was riveted to the medallion around her neck. The one that had the exact same design as the brand that had killed Maci Masterson.

Chapter Four

*D*ax stared at the medallion in the picture, dread settling in his gut. There was no denying the design was the same one, though that didn't mean that Phoebe had killed Maci. And even if she did, he was certain she had a good reason. Phoebe wasn't in the habit of killing anyone if she didn't have to. She much preferred to haul them into the Void and let the powers that be decide their fate.

He took a moment to sift through Phoebe's jewelry, looking for anything that had the same design. The pile was mostly costume jewelry he recognized from Phoebe's many disguises. There was nothing of interest there, unless... He pulled open the bottom drawer of a jewelry box and found a tray of neatly displayed rings and earrings. They were all silver, some of them slightly tarnished, all of them with ornate designs. These were old, family pieces that had been passed down from her grandmother, the ones that held spells.

Phoebe came from a powerful line of witches. Spelled family jewelry items were some of her best defenses, but he hadn't believed she ever used death spells... until now. The piece all the way on the far right was a ring with the exactly same design that had been branded into Maci's neck.

"Fuck," he muttered. That meant she'd come home if the ring was just sitting there. He frowned. Why would she come back to the house and leave again without contacting Dax or even Willow? It didn't make sense. Not at all sure the ring wasn't still spelled, Dax pulled out a pair of gloves and used them to remove the ring from the tray. He then wrapped it in a handkerchief he carried with him and shoved it in his pocket.

There was no reason to wait for her at her house. If she didn't feel safe there, she was definitely in one of her safe houses she kept around the city. Dax knew of two but was positive there were more. Just in case she did decide to come back, Dax hastily scribbled her a note, left it on her dresser, and took off.

An hour later, he'd been to two of her safe houses, left two more notes, and was sitting in front of the shotgun double he shared with Leo, half convinced that Phoebe had been abducted by Maci Masterson's friends or family. He had to find out what happened to Maci, and from there he was certain the investigation would lead him back to his girl.

Too impatient to even go into the house, Dax picked up his phone and texted Leo.

It's investigation time. I'm waiting in the car outside.

The reply was instantaneous. *On my way.*

The door swung open and the light-haired shifter bounded out of the house. He was young, early twenties, with his whole life ahead of him. Dax felt like he should warn the kid of what a lifetime of working for the Void would do to him, but he knew he'd just be wasting his breath. The kid had lost his girlfriend recently because of a shitty vampire dealer. Leo had made it his mission to be on the side of good for the city of New Orleans, and for better or worse, that meant working for the Void.

"What's going on," he asked as he slipped into the passenger side of Dax's Trooper.

"We've got a homicide to solve and a witch to find. If we find one, I think we'll solve the other." Dax put the Trooper in gear and sped down the street.

"Who's the witch?" Leo asked. "Anyone we know?"

Dax tightened his grip on his steering wheel and nodded. "Yeah. It's Phoebe. And she's in trouble."

"Shit. *Again?*" Leo asked, his blue eyes wide with disbelief. "But she just left the infirmary. Isn't she supposed to be taking it easy or something?"

"One would think," Dax said dryly.

But Leo didn't answer him. They both fell silent as Dax sped through the streets of New Orleans and toward the scene of the crime. It would have been better if he'd had enough notice to check it out before the scene was cleaned up. There wouldn't be much to see, but he needed a point of reference, and one never knew what the first-round investigators might miss. Plus he had the pictures and could get a feel for what might have gone down.

"Do you really think Phoebe did this?" Leo asked. "Seems like she would've called you at the very least."

Dax nodded, trying to ignore the unease in his gut. "Yeah, she would've. Unless she couldn't."

"You mean...?" Leo visibly swallowed, clearly catching on. "You think someone is holding her against her will?"

"No idea, really, but it's a possibility." He didn't want to think about the alternatives. If she was being held captive somewhere, at least she was alive.

"Okay, but who would do that? King is dead," Leo said, referring to the shifter who'd tried to turn both Leo and Dax into supershifters just last week. "His pack is disbanded, and I heard Glacier is being taken over by the Barré dynasty."

"Those East Coast vamps? The ones into solar and green energy? They're the ones taking over King's operation?" Dax asked, surprised.

"The very same. They saw opportunity here in the Gulf Coast and want to expand. If it works out, the Barrés will likely clean up that company, and it will be a very good thing for New Orleans."

"Huh." Dax hadn't seen that one coming. "That's good, I guess. Although Allcot won't be pleased." Not that Dax cared. He had an uneasy alliance with Allcot at the moment, but that didn't mean Dax liked the guy.

Leo let out a grunt. "Nope. But the Barrés can take care of themselves. Whatever happens, the two can battle it out privately."

"Famous last words," Dax said, knowing that wasn't how things ever worked. "The Void doesn't stay out of anything. You should know that going in."

"Right." Leo frowned. "Well, if the Barrés are as upstanding as the rumors, maybe they'll have a positive impact on this town."

"One can hope." Dax steered the Trooper onto Magazine Street in the Garden District. It was early summer, but the heat was already oppressive, causing the tourists to lie low. And considering it was just after noon, most of the paranormal community hadn't poked their heads out either.

Good. Dax didn't need an audience. "Leo, grab the folder from the back seat and check the location of the attack."

The other shifter reached behind him, grabbed the paperwork, and a second later rattled off the address. "Sixth and Coliseum. Near the cemetery."

Of course. Dax nearly rolled his eyes at the cliché. He parked under a large oak tree and hopped out. Leo followed and they made their way over to the entrance. Maci had been found just to the left of the gates. Glancing around, Dax noted there wasn't any obvious evidence that a woman had been killed there the night before. Why would there be? The pictures didn't show any blood or even signs of a struggle. Maci had just been lying there, her eyes wide open with a brand on her neck.

"Doesn't look like we're going to find anything here," Leo said.

"Maybe, maybe not," Dax said as he crouched down and inhaled deeply. The vague, rotten scent of decay filled his senses along with something that smelled like a hint of jasmine. He glanced around, looking for the vine. It was a popular one in the city, but he didn't see any in the nearby vicinity. Was it a scent Maci wore? He stood straight again and took a chance, walking up the sidewalk toward Prytania Street. The decay scent started to fade, but the jasmine was still there. "This way."

Leo rushed to catch up with his mentor. "You smell something?"

Dax nodded, scanning the area, looking for anything unusual. The sidewalk was uneven in places with vegetation debris in the street near the curb. There wasn't anything to see, nothing out of the ordinary, but then he spotted just a glimpse of red fabric poking out from beneath an old VW Bug with a flat tire that looked like it hadn't moved in weeks.

When Dax bent down to grab the fabric, the jasmine scent intensified a tiny bit, but it was also tinged with what he could only describe as fear. Like it had soured or something. He picked up a knitted sweater, the short kind that only covers the top of a woman's torso, and pressed it to his nose. The jasmine, the fear, they were both there, but he also smelled something else.

Phoebe. Her scent signature was all over the sweater. He glanced at Leo. "Phoebe was here."

"You're sure?" Leo asked, taking the sweater from Dax.

"I'm sure."

Leo took one whiff and grimaced. "Now what, boss? If someone snatched her, we need to alert Director Halston, don't we?"

"If she was snatched, yeah. But if she wasn't…" Dax let out a low growl, hating his choices. "If she's hiding out, she has a good reason, and I don't want to alert anyone who might be looking for her. But if she was taken by someone, then we need all the help we can get in finding her."

"We can look for her car, right?" Leo said. "Report it as stolen or something? At least get an idea of where she left it last?"

Dax mulled Leo's suggestion over in his mind. It was a good one. Phoebe would've probably tried to leave it somewhere where it wouldn't be noticed. He didn't think finding it would lead him right to her, but there would be valuable clues as to where she'd gone or what might have happened to her. He pulled out his phone and placed a call to the Void. When he was done, he led Leo back to the Trooper.

"Now what?" Leo asked.

"Time to meet the family of the victim. Find out why Phoebe felt she had to kill this girl." The words were like ash in his mouth. Phoebe wasn't a shifter killer. For her to end this girl, she must've feared for her life. But the lack of evidence of a struggle weighed on him. He knew there had to be an explanation, he just couldn't see a path to a reasonable one.

Chapter Five

"Ready for this?" Seth asked me.

We were sitting in a nondescript black SUV a few blocks off Frenchmen Street in the Marigny. The neighborhood was almost identical to the world I'd left behind, with century-old homes that were painted every color of the rainbow. Allcot and his vampires were already out casing the neighborhood. We were waiting for his signal.

"Not really. But if it means saving a bunch of women from a life of forced sex work, then you know I'll do whatever it takes."

"Thanks," he said and glanced out the window. After a moment he turned to me, his dark eyes piercing me. "I'm glad you're here."

I sucked in a deep breath and closed my eyes. I wasn't at all. "You know my friends back home are missing me, Seth. I can't even imagine what they're thinking right now. Willow, Tal, Dax." My voice cracked on my partner's name. "What if my doppelgänger is pretending to be me? What if she's taken my place and I'm never going to get home?"

"You will," he insisted.

Something struck me that I hadn't considered before. I'd been too freaked out by the sudden changes to really think it through. "Are you and the other Phoebe close?"

He shrugged. "Not especially."

"But in this world, she's your sister. That must mean something to you," I pressed.

"Yes and no." He shook his head. "You're my sister, Phoebe. The one I grew up with, the one I know inside and out, my real family. The Phoebe in this world... She's different. She looks like you, but who you are as people... your experiences have been totally different. They mold who a person ends up being. If you're asking if she replaced you, the answer is no. She never could."

A pain in my gut eased at his words, and I couldn't help but feel slightly stupid for worrying about how he felt about me when my entire life was turned upside down. But I had spent years looking for him while he'd spent years hiding from me and everyone else.

I understood his reasoning for living in this world. His son was here. Pandora was here, whom he seemed to love very much. While he and his son Lex could cross over, she couldn't. And even if something happened to the other Pandora, making it possible for her to cross, there would be nothing in that world that would keep Eadric Allcot away from her. It just hurt that Seth hadn't felt he could be honest and had chosen to let me believe he was missing, or worse—dead.

"I can't stay here," I said quietly. "Dax, Willow, if they haven't figured it out already, they'll do everything in their power to find me."

"I know. They love you."

"They're my family now."

He nodded. "Don't worry, Phoebe. I'll take care of it. If she hasn't come back by the time we finish with this raid, I'll go find her and bring her back myself."

Gods. I'd had no idea how much I wanted to hear those words until he actually said them. "Thank you," I said, air whooshing out of my lungs as if I'd been holding my breath. "I'm sorry I put you in this position."

"You have nothing to apologize for." His phone buzzed, and after he checked the message, he said, "Time to roll."

We both jumped out of the SUV and then took our time strolling toward Frenchmen Street. I'd used some of my talents to disguise us so that we didn't give ourselves away. Today we were dressed as tourists. I was wearing linen capris and a matching tank top while Seth was in jeans and a tacky T-shirt with a giant crawfish on the front. The words I SUCKED HEADS IN NEW ORLEANS were scrawled across the bottom. I'd tucked my dark hair under a long, honey-blond wig, but Seth had refused the blond-tipped wig I'd suggested for him. Instead, he'd gone with a Saints cap, which I had to admit made him blend right in.

"Tell me again who Genevieve is," I said. I knew she was the one who was helping us get into Clio's operation, but I hadn't been clear on what she did for the witch.

"She's the person who looks after the staff, makes sure they're up to Clio's standards. A manager of sorts. But what she really does is keep an eye on them and keep them safe. You were friends with her when you used to work at the club," Seth said. "You were friends until Allcot paid out your contract and brought you back to the plantation."

I nearly stopped dead in my tracks. "The other Phoebe was a sex worker, and Allcot *bought* her?"

Seth nodded as if he hadn't just dropped a bombshell in my lap. "He saved her actually."

And now she owed him. Was that why she'd married him? Out of obligation? It made me sick to think about my other self having so few choices that she grabbed her chance at my life the first chance she got. "He doesn't deserve her," I said defiantly.

"You might be right, but he was way better than the alternative." Seth put his finger to his lips, indicating our conversation was over, and gestured to the building in front of us. I almost laughed out loud. The Red Door. In my reality, the club was owned by Allcot and was a vampire jazz bar. Only in that world, the door was actually painted blue, while this one was red.

At least I knew the layout.

"I'll take the front. You take the back," Seth said.

I nodded. It was time to work. Being that we were the only witches in Allcot's gang, we were responsible for casting illusion spells so that the vampires could enter the club undetected to the naked eye. The spells were simple enough that the magic wouldn't be immediately detected by the witch leader. But it also meant she could break through them without much difficulty. We'd need to be on our toes.

As Genevieve had promised, the gate to get into the side of the building and to the back was unlocked. I slipped through silently while imagining the space void of any people, vampires, or werewolves and whispering a spell under my breath. Magic tingled on my skin as I sank onto a wooden swing, my limbs becoming light when the spell filtered over the brick courtyard.

And then I settled in to wait.

Allcot and his band of vampires would be entering the

building through the front. Or at least that was the plan, but less than a minute had gone by before I spotted Kai and Paxton striding toward me. But without even a flick of their gaze or a wave of acknowledgment, they pulled the back door open and hurried inside.

They hadn't seen me. That was obvious. Good, the spell was working.

I sat with my hands in my lap, trying not to fidget. Sitting on the sidelines wasn't something I was used to. I placed my hand at my waist and grabbed the hilt of my dagger, ready just in case the shit hit the fan.

"Phoebe, look out!" a voice called from seemingly out of nowhere, startling me into action just as a ball of fire came right at me. Without any thought, I dove to the ground and rolled, coming up on my feet with my dagger in my hand. The swing I'd been sitting on was engulfed in flames, radiating an intense heat that caused the flames to turn blue.

"I should've killed you the first night you came to me." The gravelly-voiced woman was right behind me, so close I could feel her breath on my neck.

"Probably," I said and jabbed my elbow into her gut before jumping out of her way.

"Stupid bitch," she said, her tone ice-cold. She had long, curly, bright red hair, silver eyes that flashed with disgust, and was holding a weapon that looked a lot like a gun.

"What are you doing to do with that?" I asked, pointing my dagger at the pistol. "Shoot me?"

Her thin lips turned into an evil smile as she started to squeeze the trigger.

I cursed and placed my hand straight out, erecting a clear shield that was like a protective barrier.

"Goodbye, Kilsen," Clio said, her smile only widening.

Magic poured into my dagger as I clutched it harder, and when I heard the bang of the gun, the weapon was already pressed against my chest, protecting my heart. The bullet sailed right through my barrier and was stopped by the magical blade, much to Clio's horror.

"How did you...? Why didn't that work?" she asked, astonished she hadn't been able to kill me. Not yet anyway. Then the strangest thing happened. Her appearance shifted into a short blonde and then a tall, thin brunette and back to the long-haired redhead.

"Magic," I growled and leaped for her, my hand closing over the gun. My attack must have surprised her, because I got the gun easily, but as soon as I took it from her, she disappeared into thin air.

I spun, searching for the witch.

Nothing. There was no one. I wasn't even sure if it had been Clio. The witch attacking me could have been anyone.

But then I heard a blood-curdling scream from inside the house. A scream I recognized.

Willow Rhoswen.

I knew she wasn't my Willow, the Willow I'd left back in my world. But she was still Willow, and leaving her to whatever fate was going on in that club was unimaginable. Holding the gun in one hand and my dagger in the other, I tore into the building.

Carnage, everywhere. A wolf was sprawled out in the hallway unmoving, a large vampire bite in his neck. A naked man was curled in the corner, blood spilling out beneath him from a wound in his gut. My stomach rolled, but the truth was I'd seen worse and probably would again.

The screaming was overhead and only louder now. I sprinted around the corner, jumping over a woman who'd fallen and was whimpering, and then took the stairs two at a time and headed straight for the office I'd known as Allcot's back in my world.

I burst through the ornate double doors and skidded to a stop, my heart in my throat. The redheaded woman I'd seen out in the courtyard was standing on the desk, her eyes narrowed as she pointed her finger at the familiar fae floating in front of her.

Willow Rhoswen.

Her wing was torn and there were shackles around both her ankles and wrists. Dried blood marred both her hands and her feet. This wasn't a new predicament for the fairy. The screaming had stopped and her head was lolling to the side, her eyes unseeing.

"Willow!" I cried and ran forward, but a bolt of magic hit me straight in the chest and hurled me back into the heavy door. My lower back hit the knob, sending a jolt of pain straight to my toes. I fell with a grunt but quickly pushed myself up and moved forward again, this time with both hands on my dagger. It could fight magic; the gun could not.

"Stand down, Kilsen," the redhead said.

"You first."

She let out a sardonic chuckle. "You always were a feisty one."

I felt my magic coil in my gut, slithering around, ready to strike.

"Don't even think about," she said with a snarl. "If you do, I'll have my man slit your brother's throat."

I jerked my attention to the two men to the left of her and almost stumbled to one knee from the shock of the sight.

My partner, Dax Marrok's, doppelgänger was holding a magic-infused knife to Seth's throat. Seth's T-shirt had been shredded by what appeared to be wolf claws, and he had four large gashes in his skin.

"Stop this, Clio," Seth ground out. "You can't win. The vampires have you surrounded."

Did they? I didn't know for sure how many vampires Allcot had enlisted for this rescue. I knew about the four from dinner, but were there more?

"They're all too busy fighting off my familiars." She turned her attention to me as her lips curved into that same chilling smiled I'd witnessed out in the courtyard. "They're immune to illusion spells. Too bad you didn't know that. You might have gotten a little farther on this fool's mission."

That wasn't quite right, I thought. Hadn't I watched Kai and Paxton go into the building without any trouble? Where were they now? Still working through the carnage downstairs? In the bar area? I had no idea.

"The only reason this one got up here is because I let him." She cut her gaze to Seth and gave Dax a nod.

He grimaced and let out a roar as he twisted Seth's arm until the entire room heard the unmistakable sound of bones cracking.

Sweat ran down Seth's face as he let out a grunt of pain and fell to the floor on one knee.

"Well done, pet," Clio said to Dax in a tone that made my stomach turn.

The shifter bared his teeth to her and growled.

She threw her head back and laughed as if all this were some big giant joke.

Dax bent his head and whispered something to Seth that sounded a lot like, "Sorry, man."

He was compelled to do her bidding. I was sure of it. His body language and the way he was glaring at Clio made that perfectly clear. If I could break her hold on him, that would give us an ally.

"Now, about Rhoswen here. She has a very special gift. I don't think it would be prudent to kill her. She's especially valuable to the vampires. How about we work out a trade," Clio said. "What do you say, Kilsen?"

The use of my name startled me. I hadn't realized she was talking to me. But that made sense, didn't it? Allcot had invaded her space, and I was Allcot's goddamned wife. It would be natural for her to assume I had bargaining power. "I'm listening," I said with a great deal more calm than I felt. She was torturing the three people I loved most in the world. Well, I loved Seth anyway. The other two were the counterparts to the people I loved, and that was good enough for me.

I took a step forward, holding her sinister gaze. "What do you have in mind?"

"Easy. I let everyone live, and you take your vamps and go." Her eyes were almost black with the power she was wielding. How long had she been levitating Willow and controlling Dax? In my universe, the prolonged use of powerful magic would drain the energy of a witch faster than just about anything else. There was no way I was taking her deal. Besides, I was pretty sure some people downstairs weren't interested in negotiating with her.

"How about you let Willow down and I'll consider it?" I asked with my eyebrows raised.

"No." She snapped her fingers, and a noose made out of silk wrapped itself around Willow's neck and tightened.

Willow's eyes popped open and she made a gurgling noise like she was choking or couldn't breathe.

"Are you ready to make that deal, Kilsen?" Clio asked.

"Don't. Do. It," Seth said.

Clio turned her ire on him and opened her mouth to no doubt order Dax to do something else vile to him, but I wasn't having it. My magic had been building the entire time I'd been standing there, and without any warning, I hurled my dagger at the witch. It moved so fast it hit her right in the middle of her chest before she even saw it coming.

Willow fell to the floor and Dax stepped back from Seth.

I knew I'd broken the spells she'd had them under, but I didn't wait to see what might happen next. The witch had already pulled the dagger from her chest, and despite the blood staining her white dress, she was moving toward me, holding my dagger high above her head, ready to use it on me.

Not so fast, witch, I thought and raised my own hand high in the air, muttering a spell under my breath. It was an ancient family one that connected precious family heirlooms to the owner. The hilt of my blade glowed yellow and then orange as it heated to unbearable levels, and finally Clio let go. It flew into my palm, cooler than an ocean breeze. As soon as I wrapped my hand around the hilt, I leaped forward, ready to take this bitch down.

But she wouldn't prove an easy mark. Before I could reach her, a locket at her throat opened all on its own and blue gas filled the room. It tasted and smelled of sulfur. My limbs turned heavy, and my mind slowed down. Sleeping gas? I didn't know for sure and I didn't care. Whatever it was, it had to go. I made a slashing motion with my dagger, forming a flaming *X* in the air. Then I poked it in the middle with the dagger, releasing the flame. It went straight for her gas, popping, crackling, and sizzling through the room as it burned her spell into nothing.

"Fuck me!" Clio cried and tried to turn and run through a side door.

But Seth was there. He grabbed her by her hair and dragged her back. She muttered curse after curse, but the fire I'd unleashed was still active and burned them all before they could be effective.

She glared at me. "That witch needs to die. I should've killed her when I had the chance."

I walked over to Seth and towered over her. "Yeah. I've heard that before." Crouching down next to her, I reached for the magical zip ties I usually kept in my back pocket and came up empty. "Dammit. Seth, do you have restraints?"

"Only ones that require spells, and I think you've managed to make those useless for the moment." He eyed the room, his gaze following the tiny sparks of fire still flying around like fireflies.

I chuckled because it was true. It was interesting. That spell didn't quite work like that at home. It didn't linger like it was doing here. I wasn't sure what to make of that.

"I'll take care of it," Allcot said from the doorway.

I glanced back at the vampire. He was disheveled, blood staining his chin, and he looked pissed off. Was that because a shifter had gashed his face or because we didn't appear to be able to handle the witch on our own? There was no telling, but before I could blink, Allcot was at Clio's side, her head in his hands. Without even a hesitation, he twisted, snapping her neck before the witch could try to utter another spell.

I gasped out loud, shocked to my core.

"Grow up, Phoebe," he said, sounding annoyed as he turned his gray eyes on me. "What did you want to happen? After what this bitch did to you, I'd think you'd be thanking me."

What she'd done to me? What did that mean? I'd have to ask Seth. "Well, I'm certainly glad she won't be torturing my friends any longer."

He glanced around the room, eyeing Willow and Seth before letting his gaze linger on Dax. Finally he gave me a withering stare and said, "*Friends?*"

"I… uh, I just meant…" I shook my head, not sure what to say. "I just meant that she can't hurt anyone anymore."

"Right." His tone was dismissive. "Take care of the fairy." Glancing back, he pointed to Dax. "You, come with me."

While I knelt next to Willow, carefully untangling the scarf from her neck, the shifter got to his feet and reluctantly moved toward the vampire. There was a scowl on his face and he looked like he was one wrong move away from ripping Allcot's head off. As they stepped through the door, I heard Allcot say, "Clean up the carnage. I want this place ready to open back up by the end of the week."

"What?" I jumped back up and moved toward Allcot. "You can't be serious? What are you going to do? Open it up as a jazz club?"

"Of course not, Phoebe. This place is a brothel and that's what it will continue to be." Allcot moved toward the door and barked at Dax, "Come."

The pair of them disappeared into the next room while I stared after him and Willow started to cry.

Chapter Six

The Masterson residence was in the Lakeview neighborhood. Dax and Leo sat in front of a large custom home with floor-to-ceiling windows in the front and ornate double wooden doors. The grounds had been manicured to perfection, with jasmine vines, large red hibiscus flowers, and a blooming crepe myrtle in the middle of the yard. Two matching BMWs were sitting in the driveway, one with a license plate that said HIS and the other said HERS. There was also a sporty powder-blue Mini Cooper off to the right.

"Wow," Leo said, his eyes wide. "Gorgeous place. A lot nicer than the double we live in with the peeling paint and sagging porch."

"Watch it, kid. It's cheap and provides a roof over your head," Dax said, pushing his door open.

"I wasn't complaining. Just making an observation." Leo waited for him on the sidewalk. "I wouldn't know what to do in a fancy place like this anyway. Can you imagine? I'd probably break that fancy door handle the first time I used it."

He probably would, Dax thought. It appeared to be crystal and looked more delicate than it likely was. "You'd be fine," he said and rang the doorbell.

Nothing. No dogs barked. No sound or movement from inside.

Dax rang again and then knocked. Leo started to crane his head to peek over the fence, but then the door swung open and a woman in a white T-shirt with a coffee stain on the front opened the door. Her tearstained face was pale, and she looked like she wanted to vomit.

"Mrs. Masterson?" Dax asked.

"We're not up for visitors," she said with a sob and started to close the door.

"Ma'am, if you'll just give us a moment of your time. We're here from the Arcane, the paranormal investigation division. We'd like to ask you a few questions about your daughter if you don't mind. The faster we gather information, the easier it will be to solve this crime."

Tears spilled from her bright green eyes as she stared at him, almost unable to function.

"Who is it?" a man called from behind her.

"Dax Marrok and Leo Shepard, Mr. Masterson. We're investigating your daughter's death."

Loud footsteps rang through the house, and a moment later a man with silver hair and sad gray eyes placed his hands on his wife's shoulders and moved her out of the way. "Let them in Vi, they have a job to do."

"What does it matter?" she choked out, her bottom lip quivering. "She's gone. Nothing will bring her back."

"We can honor her memory by bringing down who did this." He waved to Dax and Leo, inviting them in.

Dax stepped into the immaculate house, noting the expensive antique furniture, fancy built-ins, and abundance of artwork on the walls. This was a well-to-do family and unlikely to be running with the underbelly of the city, but looks could be deceiving. He'd keep an open mind.

"I'm sorry to intrude on you and your wife so soon after hearing the news this morning. I wouldn't be here if there was any choice in the matter," Dax said to Mr. Masterson.

"I understand," he said with a tired sigh, leading them to the informal kitchen table. "Have a seat. Would you like something? Coffee? Water? Iced tea?"

"No. Thank you," Dax said while Leo shook his head and added, "I'm fine."

The silver-haired man went to work pouring a cup of coffee and then got a glass of water. He put the water in front of his wife and sat at the end of the table, holding the mug with both hands. "You're here from the Arcane?"

Dax nodded. He didn't want to say the Void. The general public didn't know much about the shadow division, and he'd just as soon keep it that way. "I'd like to ask some questions if you don't mind."

"Go ahead. Let's get this over with."

"Thanks, Mr. Masterson," Dax started.

"Call me Colin."

"Thanks, Colin." Dax pulled a small notepad from his pocket and flipped it open. "Can you tell me about your daughter? Did she work? What else did she do? Was she involved in your charity projects or anything?"

"She worked and went to school," Colin said. "She just

started graduate school at Tulane for an architecture degree this year, and she worked at a design firm in the Garden District."

Dax nodded and jotted that down. "Any problems at school or work that you know of?"

He shook his head. As it turned out, she was a straight-A student. And the place she worked, she'd been there for four years, working for her best friend's mother. There was less than zero indication that anything was suspicious about Maci's school or work life.

Dax asked about other shifters she might've hung out with, any packs she was involved with, or any other paranormals like vampires or witches.

"I'm the leader of our pack, Mr. Marrok. We tend to stay out of vampire/shifter politics and prefer to stay community oriented. Most of Maci's friends are the kids in our youth group. None of them have been in trouble. We have no idea why a witch would come after our daughter." He nodded to a picture on the wall beside him. It was one of him, his wife, and a very vibrant Maci. She had a huge smile on her face and her eyes sparkled with life. "That was taken at Christmas."

It was hard to imagine such a girl being involved in anything that would justify Phoebe killing her. Dax swallowed a lump in his throat and continued the interview. A half hour later, he had the names of her closest friends but absolutely nothing to go on. The Mastersons were model citizens. Colin Masterson was involved in three different charities. One for funding a soup kitchen, another for raising money for college for low-income students, and the last one funded the local public hospital. The Mastersons were nothing short of saints in this city.

As they were leaving, Dax handed the man his card. "If you find or hear of anything that makes you uneasy or suspicious that could've led to foul play, please don't hesitate to call me."

"Sure, son," the man said, his face gaunt with grief.

"I'm very sorry for your loss. Trust me when I say we'll do our best to get to the bottom of this." Dax shook the man's hand and felt sick. Something wasn't adding up.

The door clicked closed behind them, and without a word Leo and Dax headed back to the Trooper.

Once they were back in the vehicle, Leo let out a slow breath. "That was brutal."

Dax just nodded and cranked the ignition.

"Now what?" Leo asked him.

He glanced over at the kid. "You know, Leo, for once I have no idea."

DAX TOOK a sip of his Mocha in Motion, the magically enhanced drink that was designed to boost your energy, and leaned forward in the overstuffed chair, staring intently at Willow Rhoswen. After he and Leo left the Mastersons' place, he hadn't consciously decided to visit the Fated Cupcake, the shop that Willow owned, but had found himself parked out front anyway.

"Have you heard from her yet?"

The fae frowned and shook her head. "She didn't come home last night. I thought she must be with you. But then when you called this morning… Did you check her safe houses?"

"Two of them. I don't know where the rest are," Dax said.

"Me neither." Willow placed her hand on her iPhone. "Have you asked Allcot?"

Dax felt a tightening in his chest at the mention of the vampire's name and shook his head. "I don't see how he could be involved in this."

Willow let out a humorless snort of laughter and brushed her strawberry blond hair out of her face. "Since when is he *not* involved in the crazy shit that happens in this town? I swear, every time something goes down, he's always in the middle of it."

She had a point. Why hadn't he thought of that?

"I can make the call," Leo said from his spot on the floor near Link's dog bed. Link, the shih tzu shifter, was in wolf form, his paws in the air, twisting back and forth while Leo rubbed his belly.

"Why you?" Dax asked.

"Why not me?" he countered. "If I'm going to be a Void agent, I'm going to need to deal with all kinds, right?"

"Sure," Dax said with a nod. "Fine. Go ahead. Ask him what he knows and if he's seen her. If he hasn't, find out if he can put the word out among his vampires that we're looking for her."

"I'm on it." He pulled out his phone and tapped a couple of buttons. Link rolled over and rested his big head on Leo's knee, nudging his hand to indicate the petting session wasn't over.

Willow laughed. "Link, stop."

The wolf turned his big head in her direction but then went right back to nudging Leo's free hand. Leo grinned down at the wolf and started stroking his ears. The wolf let out a contented sigh and relaxed.

It took Leo a few tries to finally find someone who could get Allcot on the phone. The kid had met Allcot a few times and had participated in a few battles against mutual enemies, but it wasn't like Leo was important enough to be on the vampire's radar. But Leo was persistent, impressing Dax with his tenacity, and eventually he got the powerful vamp to talk to him.

When Leo ended the call, he said, "Allcot hasn't seen her. But he did say he'll send out a directive to his employees that they are to contact him if anyone sees her. He said he'd let us know right away."

"That's probably going to be a lot faster than waiting for the Void to track down her car," Dax said.

Willow worried the edge of her apron. "Did you call it in stolen or something?"

Dax nodded. "I need to find her as soon as possible. It was the only thing I could think of at the time."

"It wasn't a bad idea," she agreed.

"It was Leo's."

Willow smiled at him. "Good thinking, Leo."

A slight flush stained his cheeks.

"All right. Let's go." Dax stood and held his hand out to Willow.

"Nun-uh," she said and opened her arms to give him a hug.

Dax welcomed her embrace. He'd been on edge ever since he'd realized Phoebe hadn't gone home the night before.

"We'll find her," Willow whispered. "I'm sure there's a good explanation. There always is."

"I know."

She released him and patted his chest like a grandmother would do when trying to soothe her grandson. "And try to remember she's a big girl and a talented witch. She'll be all right."

"Yeah she will," Leo chimed in. "Phoebe is a badass."

Dax said nothing. He knew she was more than capable. He was her partner. He knew that side of her better than any of them. No, he wasn't worried about her safety; he was starting to worry about what she might have done and why. "Thanks again, Willow."

"Sure. If you need my help with anything or need Link for backup, you know where to find us," she said as she opened the side door that led to the street instead of her bakery.

"Seriously?" Leo glanced once more at Link. "You'd let us borrow him?"

She glanced at her wolf who was sitting right beside her, watching the two men leave. "Sure. If you need him. He comes in very handy sometimes."

"Awesome. Thanks, Willow," Leo said and waved as they made their way back out into the oppressive summer heat.

Dax climbed into his Trooper, but instead of taking off, he just sat there thinking.

"What is it?" Leo asked him.

"I'm trying to decide where I'd go if I were Phoebe." He bit down on his bottom lip, running the past few weeks through his mind. When she hadn't been looking for him, she'd been looking for her brother. Did she have any leads? Yes. In fact, he'd been the one to give it to her. Someone had told him her brother had been spotted out on River Road.

Had she gone out there with just that little bit of information? Knowing her, he'd say she most definitely had.

He started the engine and took off, heading toward the highway.

"Where are we going?" Leo asked when they got on the bridge headed toward the west bank.

"To track down my girl."

Chapter Seven

I was fuming. Pure unadulterated rage was surging through my veins. Willow Rhoswen was lying in a bed made of the finest linens as a healer tended to her raw wrists and ankles while I paced, plotting a way to murder Eadric Allcot.

How was it possible an even worse version of that vampire existed in an alternate reality? At least back at home he had someone he cared about enough that he retained some humanity. It was pretty clear that whatever he'd had with my doppelgänger had never come close to what he had with Pandora.

"Phoebe?" Willow said, her voice weak after being strangled with a scarf.

"Yes, Wil?" I said, moving to sit on the edge of her bed.

"Thank you," she croaked out. "You did it. You really did it."

"Did what?" I asked, confused.

"You saved me. You said you would and you did." She reached out and squeezed my hand. The healer had wrapped both wrists with white gauze and cleaned her hands of the dried blood. She already looked a hundred times better... except for the bruising around her neck. Her lips were cracked from what I assumed was dehydration, but she smiled at me anyway. "Now we can be free."

The pit in my stomach grew. How was I going to tell her she'd traded one captor for another? I couldn't. I had to convince Allcot that the only right thing to do was to help these women get on their feet and find good jobs, not exploit them further.

"Gods, I hope so," I said and stormed out of the room, intent on finding the man I was supposedly married to. Just the thought made me gag. The sounds of footsteps filtered up the stairs, followed by evidence of furniture being moved. Someone was crying in the room just to my left. I paused, unsure if I should check on the weeping woman or keep going until I found Allcot.

Definitely find Allcot first. I had to, while I was still fueled by pure anger. Only I had no idea where he was. Willow had been taken to a room at the other end of the hall, and it sounded as if the rooms near hers were occupied. That left the downstairs or the wing where I'd first found Clio.

Since I was upstairs, I decided to try Clio's office first. The doors were closed, but when I pushed on the right one, it opened with ease. I glanced around at the broken chair to the left, the bloodstains on the rug to the right, and the piles of paperwork that had been scattered all over the room. The place looked like a tornado had hit it. But there was no one there. Not even Clio's corpse. *Thank goodness for small favors.*

I turned to go but paused when the door swung open and Dax walked in.

A look of surprise lit his handsome face, but then he scowled. "What are you doing in here?"

"Uh, I was looking for Allcot," I said. "I wanted—"

"Your *husband* is downstairs, forcing the girls to sign new contracts. You should probably join him before he finds us breathing the same air." He dropped the bucket he was holding, pulled out a trash bag, and started to gather the garbage.

I stood there, stunned at the pure hatred I'd heard in his tone. I supposed I couldn't blame him for being angry. Allcot had treated him like a dog. And if he really was forcing the women into new contracts, then the vampire was truly vile. But I didn't have anything to do with that.

You're married to him, the voice in my head said.

"Shit!" I muttered and moved toward Dax. When I was near, I reached out to touch his arm, but he flinched away.

"Don't touch me," he snarled, his dark eyes flashing gold.

I stepped back, startled. "I'm sorry. I just... I wanted to say I don't agree with anything Allcot is doing."

He stared at me for a long moment. Then he shook his head and went back to work on cleaning up the mess. "Does it matter, Phoebe? You're with him now. You can't just turn back time."

"What's that supposed to mean?" I asked. "I'm still my own person. Just because I'm..." I couldn't even say the words. "Allcot doesn't own me."

Dax let out a bark of laughter. "Is that what you're telling yourself?"

"Hey!" I took a step closer, getting in his face. "No one owns me."

"No? Clio did until he bought you off her. So what? You think because you wear his ring it's any different? It's not like when we were kids, Phoebe. We're both obligated to that bastard, and whatever you're hoping to get out of me, just fucking forget it, all right? I've already lost enough." He turned away from me and let out a growl as he kicked a chair out of the way.

"Not like when we were kids?" I asked, unable to get the words out of my head. Had we been friends in this world?

"Fuck." He turned his tortured eyes on me, and I swear I saw more vulnerability in him than I ever had with my Dax. Not even when we both thought he was dying and his days were numbered.

"Why are you so angry?" I asked, my voice so low I wasn't even sure he could hear me. I was certain my doppelgänger would know, but seeing him so tortured was nearly ripping my heart out. All I wanted to do was wrap my arms around him and reassure him that we'd beat Allcot at whatever game he was playing. But I couldn't do that. I had some sort of history with this Dax, that was certain. But did we trust each other? Clearly not. Maybe we had at one time, but not now. I was married to a man we both hated, only Dax had no way of knowing my true feelings.

He stood up straight and pierced me with his glare. "You're not that stupid, Phoebe. I know you did what you had to do. But that doesn't mean you didn't rip my heart right out of my chest when you walked away from me and into the arms of Allcot."

I opened my mouth to deny that I'd ever do anything even remotely like what he'd described. But there was no truth to those words in this reality. I wasn't my doppelgänger, and it appeared that she had done exactly what he'd just accused me of doing. And according to my brother, she was trying to start a family with a shitty vampire. Or was she? She'd left, hadn't she? The more I learned about her life, the more I couldn't blame her. I just hoped she wasn't making a mess of my life back in my reality, because I fully intended to get back there, sooner rather than later.

Instead, I frowned and just said, "I'm sorry, Dax."

He held my unflinching gaze for a few beats before turning and disappearing from the room without saying a word.

"Dammit." That had hurt more than I cared to admit. It was hard to look at the doppelgänger of the man I loved and not feel *everything*.

"Have a nice visit?"

I jerked my head up and found myself staring into the steel-gray eyes of Eadric Allcot. He was leaning against the doorframe, his arms crossed over his chest as if he was patiently watching me. But I knew better. His jaw was tight and his eyes slightly narrowed. He was pissed.

"No. Not really," I said, tired of playing the game.

"I never did understand what you saw in him." He pushed off the frame and strolled in, kicking the door closed behind him. "He was never destined to be anything more than a servant."

"Why?" My entire body was rigid as I watched him come closer, stalking me as if I were prey.

He didn't answer. Instead, he grabbed me by the chin and twisted my neck, exposing the bite marks from the night before. "You remember these, right, love?"

How could I forget?

He reached up and brushed his thumb over the two puncture wounds.

A shiver ran through me, reminding me of the pleasure

I'd felt while he'd been feeding from me, and I swear my entire body swayed toward him completely against my will.

"Yes, you definitely do remember," he whispered and pressed his cool lips against my neck.

Tears of pure frustration stung the backs of my eyes, and I tried to force myself to move away from him, to take a step back so that I could get my bearings again. Instead, I tilted my head, giving him even more access.

He let out a soft chuckle. "That's right. You want my lips on you, don't you? Just like the whore you used to be, you'll do anything for just a moment of pure bliss, the kind of bliss only my fangs can provide."

Just like the whore you used to be...

His words shook me to the core. Dax had said something similar. That Clio had owned me until Allcot had purchased me, and now he was calling me a whore. Is that how I'd known Willow? Had I worked for Clio at the brothel? The idea made bile rise in the back of my throat.

"Come on, Phoebe," Allcot said. "Want to try for that baby right here on Clio's old desk?" His hands moved to my hips, pulling me closer so that I was molded against his rock-hard body.

I glared up at him, hating every inch of him. He might have purchased the other Phoebe and married her, but Dax was right. He still thought of her—and now me—as property. I pressed both hands to his chest and shoved him back. Or at least I tried to. He was so solid he barely moved. But it was enough for me to slip out of his grip and step away from him. "I think baby making is off the table."

He raised a skeptical eyebrow. "I thought you wanted kids?"

"With you?" I spat out before I could stop myself. "Not

after the way you threw me across the room last night and not since you've unilaterally decided to force the girls into new contracts. I thought we were freeing them from this place. If I'd known you were just going to take over for Clio, I never would've agreed to this."

Confusion flashed over his stony features, but then it was replaced with amusement. "You thought they were going to go on to marry their princes? That they'd all end up living in a plantation home where their husbands give them everything they could possibly want? And then be ungrateful, just like you?"

"Ungrateful?" I huffed, horrified by his worldview. Had he just implied that the only thing these women might want out of life was a husband to take care of them? "Perhaps if I wasn't married to an abuser, things would be different."

He let out a sigh and strode over to the desk, taking a seat in the leather chair. "Let's get a few things straight, wife of mine."

"Fine. Let's." I wasn't backing down. I'd never been afraid of the Allcot in my world. I sure as hell wasn't going to be afraid of this one.

"First of all, I'm not forcing anyone to sign the new contract. That's entirely up to them. They are free to stay, with better working conditions, I might add, or pack up their things and go. And secondly, if you don't want to be married to me, you're free to go as well. But you won't see your brother or your nephew, and you won't take anything with you. The door is open. All you have to do is walk through it."

The desire to storm out of the room was strong. There was nothing I'd have liked better than to get out from under Allcot's thumb. But I didn't have that luxury. I couldn't leave his plantation home. That's where the tear in the universe was. And Seth was there. Not to mention I liked Pandora. I needed to stick close so that I was ready to go when Seth brought my doppelgänger back. Besides, I didn't want to make any big decisions for her. If Allcot was making me this offer, there was no reason to believe he wouldn't make her the same one. That was her choice, not mine.

"I'll stay," I said, holding that gaze, refusing to back down. "But intimacy is off the table for the time being."

His lips curved into a knowing smile. "Sure, love. Whatever you say."

He'd agreed, but by the way he was gazing at the bite marks on my neck, it was obvious he thought he knew exactly how this was going to play out. Well, he could think anything he wanted. There was no way in hell I'd be sleeping with Eadric Allcot.

"Did you offer the women any money to get back on their feet?" I asked.

He blinked at me, and I had the feeling he'd been taken off guard by my question. "Why exactly would I do that?"

"Because it's the right thing to do." I crossed my arms over my chest again and added, "Do you have any idea what it's like to be out in the world with literally nothing? Of course you don't," I answered for him. "These women, all they know is this place. Their choice is to leave the place they've called home for who knows how long and their friends to live out on the streets, or to stay here and sign your new contract. I don't know what it says, but I guarantee you it's better than sleeping under a bench and begging for food because they have no means to support themselves. Asking them to make this choice is just as immoral as forcing them to work here."

"So what exactly would you have me do?" he asked,

tilting his head to the side. "Just give them handouts, send them on their way, and then hire other young women who have no other prospects?"

"How about you keep them on as waitstaff instead of sex workers?"

His eyebrows shot up. "The place will close down within a week. All the vamps who frequent this place will leave for the brothel up the street, and we'll have to shut down. Your friends will be on the street anyway."

Would they? Did this world really work that way? I just didn't know enough about it to know what opportunities there were for women. It seemed like women's rights were closer to the early twentieth century rather than the twenty-first that I lived in.

Allcot stood up. "This conversation is over. If you want to help your friends find a new life, that's on you. Do whatever you want. But stay away from that shifter. He owes me, and I plan to collect."

"What do you mean, he *owes* you?" I asked, narrowing my eyes.

"Never mind." He strode over to the door and yanked it open. But before he left, he glanced over his shoulder and said, "I mean it, Phoebe. If I find out you're involved with him, I'll kill him. Remember that before you decide to betray me."

Chapter Eight

"What are you looking for?" Leo asked, peering out the windshield of the Trooper at the large white plantation house gleaming in the summer sun.

"I'm not sure," Dax said. "Phoebe's Charger. Her brother. Any magical shops that either of them would've stopped at. Short of those, I guess we can start showing her picture around, see if anyone's seen her."

Leo leaned back in his seat. "This is a wild-goose chase, isn't it?"

"Probably. But what else are we going to do? We don't have any other leads." Dax pushed his door open and climbed out.

After speaking to the owner and learning nothing, he climbed back into the vehicle and stopped at three more plantations. No one had talked to a pretty brunette or seen a gunmetal-gray Charger roaming around River Road.

Frustrated, he turned the Trooper around and started to head back to the city. "This was a stupid idea."

"No it wasn't." Leo shook his head. "Like you said, we

don't have any other leads. Isn't this what investigators do when they're stumped on a case?"

"I guess," Dax grumbled, knowing the kid was right. He just felt so fucking helpless.

"Turn here," Leo said, pointing to a dirt road.

Dax slowed and was already turning right when he asked, "Why? The place looks deserted."

"Exactly. What if Phoebe's hiding out there?" Leo asked.

The dilapidated plantation was in bad shape. Part of the roof was missing, windows were broken, the columns were in serious decay, and the upstairs balcony seemed to be barely holding on. Considering it was hotter than Hades outside and the place clearly had no electricity, the chances of Phoebe hiding out there were next to nil. And yet Dax couldn't deny that something was pulling him toward the place, like he needed to be there.

Leo jumped out first and followed the tire tracks closer to the house. Dax followed, feeling the back of his neck prickle like someone was watching them. He glanced around, finding no one. All that was left of the place was the decaying home and a few trees. Behind the house there appeared to be some old shacks that were being reclaimed by the earth.

"Dax, look," Leo said, pointing to the ground.

The shifter moved forward, frowning. "What am I looking at?"

"The footsteps. See them close to the tire tracks? They go for about ten feet and then disappear, as if the person just vanished or floated away."

Dax crouched down and inspected the prints. They were boot tracks, kind of narrow and on the small side. It was impossible to know if they belonged to a male or female, but he was guessing someone petite, likely a female. "Maybe the person was a shifter and shifted into wolf form."

"No wolf tracks," Leo said. "Vampire that can levitate?"

"Could be." Dax stood and followed the tracks back to the car. "There are more that come from here. Different shoes, but it's clear this second person got into the driver's seat."

Leo took a look and nodded. "You're right about that. Curious."

It was curious, but other than petite footprints, there wasn't anything to indicate the person who'd been there was Phoebe. Dax sighed and ran a hand down his face in frustration. They were getting nowhere. "Come on. This doesn't tell us anything."

"What about this?" Leo bent down, brushed some dirt back, and retrieved a necklace with a silver locket. He held it up, studying it.

Dax's breath caught. It couldn't be Phoebe's, could it? She definitely wore one most of the time. It contained a sleeping spell she used when she needed it. He reached out and took it from Leo. After wiping the locket with his shirt, he stared down at the engraved tree of life on the oval pendant and sucked in a hard breath. "It's hers."

"Holy shit," Leo said. "What are the chances? I mean, I was just standing here and spotted something glinting in the sun."

Dax wasn't listening. He was eyeing the house, wondering if Leo had been onto something. Had she stayed there? It might explain the reason he felt drawn to the old place. Without saying a word, he made his way to the structure. The front door was boarded up, but the third window on the right was completely gone. He stepped through and eyed the interior. It was full of dust and debris. Small animal tracks were visible in the large sitting room. It was clear from the first glance she hadn't been inside.

He turned and found Leo on his heels. "She isn't here."

"I know." He held up the phone Dax had left in the console of the Trooper. "You got a text from Allcot. Phoebe was spotted in town at Howler's."

Dax frowned. "The shifter bar on Basin?"

Leo nodded.

What the hell? Dax grabbed his phone, read the message that was still displayed, and cursed. What was she doing? Tracking someone? Why wouldn't she call? Dax pulled up his contacts and hit her name. The call went straight to voice mail. He shoved Phoebe's locket into his pocket and said, "Looks like we need to get to Howler's."

DUE TO AFTERNOON TRAFFIC, it took over an hour to get back to the city. By the time Dax parked the Trooper, he was vibrating with impatience. He jumped out of the vehicle and took off without waiting for Leo.

"Whoa, dude," Leo said as he caught up to him. "You look like you're wound so tight you're ready to snap."

"Wouldn't you be if your girl was MIA?" Dax snapped.

"I would… if I had a girl." He hung his head and quickened his pace.

Shit, Dax thought, hating himself for being so careless. Leo's girlfriend had died not long ago from a bad batch of drugs that King had been pushing to the shifters around the city. Justice had been served to that bastard, but it hadn't brought Leo's girl back.

"Hey, Leo." He jogged to catch up with him. "I'm sorry, man. I'm just losing my mind trying to figure out what's going on."

Leo gave Dax a short nod. "I know. Don't worry about it. You can't walk on eggshells around me for the rest of your life. I'm just gonna have to figure out how to deal."

"Yeah, but I don't need to be a dick in the meantime."

"You aren't." Leo gave him a half-hearted smile.

"I just hope she's still there, that's all. It took way too long to get back into town."

"At least we know she's all right. That's something," Leo said, reaching for the door of the bar.

"You got that right. I just hope there's a damned good explanation."

"Bad Moon Rising" blared from the bar's sound system as Dax stood near the door, letting his eyes adjust to the darkness. It was happy hour and the place was starting to fill up, but with one scan of the room, Dax knew Phoebe wasn't there. It was more of a feeling than the fact that he didn't see her right away, and it unsettled him. Phoebe was his partner and his girlfriend. He hadn't even told her he loved her yet. Did he? It wasn't something he'd admitted to himself yet, much less to anyone else. Yet, without her by his side, he felt like he was missing a piece of himself. And he knew without a doubt that the piece he needed was not in that bar.

"She's not here," Dax told Leo through clenched teeth.

"Give me a minute," Leo said and headed over to the bar to talk to the pink-haired shifter tending bar.

Dax paced the floor, holding on to the back of his neck with one hand. *Now what?* He asked himself. He needed to calm the fuck down, that's what. He needed to be doing exactly what Leo was doing, which was interviewing the bartender and the customers to see if they'd seen or talked to her. An ache formed in his gut, and it didn't take a genius to figure out why. He'd gone from worrying something had to happened to her to suspecting her of a heinous crime.

He wanted to scream, *Why, Phoebe?*

Why hadn't she called? Why was she letting herself be seen in a shifter bar if she didn't want to be found? She had to know he'd hear about it. Maybe she was waiting outside right at that moment just so she could connect? He spun and walked out, scanning the area. Nothing.

The door opened and Leo strode out.

Dax turned to him expectantly. "Did they know anything?"

He shrugged one shoulder. "Not really. She was here for about twenty minutes, managed to get another shifter to buy her two drinks, and then left with him."

Cold jealousy seeped into his gut. "Another shifter? Who?"

"She said he's some dude from Uptown. She only knows him as Knox. Said he's a clean-cut guy who's runs some sort of nonprofit in the city."

"Nonprofit, huh?" That sounded an awful lot like someone who would run in the Mastersons' circles. "All right. Let's go. We have some research to do."

Leo gave him a questioning glance but didn't say a word as he fell in step beside his mentor. "Are we headed home?"

Dax shook his head. "Back to the office."

Twenty minutes later, they were sitting in the office Dax shared with Phoebe, scanning shifter files.

"What am I looking for?" Leo asked.

"A member of the Masterson pack who goes by Knox. First name, last name, nickname," Dax took a sip of coffee and turned a page of the research he'd printed out. He wanted to know if there were any skeletons in the Masterson pack. There was likely a very good reason Phoebe was lying low. He just needed to find it. He flipped the page again and sat up straighter, suddenly very interested in his reading material.

"Find something?" Leo asked.

"Yes. Look at this." He slid a single sheet over to Leo. "What do you see?"

Leo pushed his files away and studied the paper. He frowned, but then his mouth dropped open into a shocked *O* before he said, "Holy shit. Are they *those* Mastersons?"

"Looks like it." Dax grabbed the paper, quickly made a copy, and said, "Let's go. We have a vampire to interview."

Chapter Nine

---

*A*llcot and I hadn't spoken for three days. In fact, he'd recruited Seth to deal with some problem in Baton Rouge that no one, not even Pandora, seemed to know the details about. The fact that Allcot wasn't around was welcome news. I couldn't say the same for Seth. When I'd found out they'd left with no ETA on their expected return, I was furious.

Pandora had said the last-minute trip was probably unavoidable. Seth didn't like to leave her unless he absolutely had to. I could see that about him. He always was the loyal type. That was one of the many reasons it'd been so hard when he'd just disappeared all those years ago. I'd spent a very long time thinking he was dead because I couldn't imagine him just taking off. But now I knew, and here I was in this fucked-up new reality, struggling to just maintain my own autonomy.

After coercing one of Allcot's vampires into giving me a ride into town, I strode into the Red Door and glanced around. The place was still in shambles after the fight that had gone down three days before, but the women were working hard on cleaning it up. There wasn't much time before the reopening on Friday night. It was just like Allcot to leave town and make his employees clean up his mess.

A couple of the women were busy filling trash bags with debris while another was clearing the bar of broken bottles and spilled booze. I planned to help, but first I wanted to check on Willow. I loved that fae more than anyone else in my world, and I couldn't help but feel protective of her in this one. I found her sitting on a large oak tree limb just outside the open window. When she saw me, she scrambled back inside, her eyes alight with joy.

"Hey," I said, smiling at her.

She rewarded me with a genuine smile and jumped up to give me a big hug. "Phoebe. I was wondering when I'd see you again."

I pulled away from her and inspected her wrists. The bandages were gone and the skin was starting to heal. "Looks like you're on the mend. How are the ankles?"

"Itchy." She lifted one foot, and I noted that the wounds were deeper there. She'd likely have scars that never went away.

"Yikes. Does the healer have any herbs that can help?"

She nodded and a dreamy look claimed her features. "Yes. He was wonderful. He applied a cream, and he gave me this." She touched a jade stone she was wearing as a pendant around her neck. "It's supposed to help channel my energy so I'll heal faster."

"Good." I glanced down at the rings on my fingers and thought of the pendant I usually wore around my neck. The rings were all spelled with powerful magic designed to take down my enemies. I couldn't help but wonder what they were doing to my energy. Nothing good, I was certain. When I got home, I'd need to remember to ask Talisen, Willow's husband, if he had something to keep me whole and grounded. He was a fae gifted in crystals and stone magic.

"It is. He was really nice too." She smiled shyly. "He told me if I ever needed a job, he might be thinking of bringing someone on to help with some herb treatments."

"What! That's great news!" I cried, grabbing her hands. "When do you start? Do you need help moving out of here?"

Her sweet face crumpled, and she shook her head. "I can't move, Phoebe. You know that."

"Why not?" I demanded. "Of course you can. I'll help you."

She frowned. "I signed a contract. I can't just leave. Allcot won't let me. You know how this goes."

I slowly sank down into a velvet chair I hadn't noticed before and took a look around. The room had been freshly painted and brand-new furniture had been moved in. Everything was elegant, very tasteful, with rich touches of fine art on the walls, lush bedding, and lots of fresh flowers and potted plants everywhere. It dawned on me that she'd chosen or been given this room because of the tree right outside. Fae got their energy from the earth. Someone was making sure she had plenty of access to the foliage she craved.

"I can talk to him," I insisted. "It's not like the place is even opened back up yet."

"But he already fixed up my room." She waved a hand, indicating the lavish surroundings. "You know I've never lived anywhere this nice. When Clio had this place, we were lucky to even get new bedding once every couple of years."

"It's just a room," I said, knowing that it was anything

but. How would I feel if I'd had nothing my entire life and suddenly a savior came in and transformed my reality into one that resembled a fairy tale? Even if that fairy tale was just another version of the grimdark tale I'd been living. "And if you worked for the healer, you wouldn't have to sell yourself for survival."

Willow just shrugged, her expression darkening. "What difference does it make, Phoebe? As sweet as the healer seemed to be, I'd likely just be trading one prison for another. Do you really think he just offered a prostitute a job and expects nothing in return? That's not how the world works, and you know it. Look what happened to you."

Her assessment of the situation made my blood boil. I wasn't mad at her, I was pissed at the repression that had gotten her to this point. And who was to say she wasn't right? I didn't even know the healer. What if he did just want her as his own personal fuck doll? I sighed. "So what's the plan? Will you just work here forever?"

"Oh no. I plan to finish out my work contract and take Allcot up on his offer to take classes at the college. Then when I get my bonus, I'll move out and see about finding a job either at a healer's office or some sort of restaurant or bakery. I always wanted to put my magic to use and see what I can do with it."

I sat back in the chair, stunned. Offer? School? Bonus? What was she talking about? The Willow I knew was especially skilled at altering herbs and making magical treats. It made sense that this one would pursue something along those lines, so her plans didn't surprise me. But the mention of an offer from Allcot floored me. "Um, Wil, what's in your contract?"

"You know, just the new standard terms. Commit to

working here for one year and Eadric will give us time off to take classes and pay for them. Then once our contract is complete, he'll give a bonus. It's large enough to pay for getting set up in a new apartment and put a little away for emergencies. Honestly, Phoebe, it's like a dream come true. A week ago, I thought I'd be working here until I aged out and Clio threw me out on the streets. Now I have a plan, something to look forward to. Eadric is going to save me. I guess just the way he saved you."

Saved me? Didn't look like it from where I was standing. Sure, he'd gotten my doppelgänger out of the prostitution business, but I didn't see where she was any better off. Still, I couldn't deny that what he was offering Willow was a thousand times better than I'd thought it would be. "Does everyone else have the same contract?"

Willow nodded. "The first one he had us sign was for five years, standard wages, but then he came back a day later and offered us these new ones. I don't know what happened or why he changed his mind, but everyone here is thrilled."

Holy fuck. I sat back, stunned. Had my words caused him to have a change of heart? It seemed likely. Why else would he have done an about-face? My vitriol toward him softened a bit, but then I remembered that the Allcot I knew had always been some sort of dichotomy of good and evil. It seemed this one was the same. In fact, it seemed that all the doppelgängers had the same basic traits as their counterparts in the competing realities.

That was good to know. It would be easier to assess people.

"I can see why," I said, squeezing her hand. "I still wish he'd just help everyone get on their feet without you having to work here though."

Willow gently shook her head and gave me a small indulgent smile. "You know that's not how this world works. It's easier if you just accept it."

"You're right." That was my friend Willow, always practical and finding her way in the murky world even when it cost her. I'd always been of two minds about her ability to navigate Allcot's world. Annoyance and admiration fought for dominance most days. She did what she had to in order to survive, often working with Allcot or his organization even when there was a moral gray area. And here she was proving she could do it again. "It would just be a hell of a lot easier to swallow if we won a few battles along the way."

"We do. This one was a win. It's not the war, but it's a battle."

I wasn't sure if I agreed with her, but at least I could see her argument. In my mind, we'd win a battle when at least some segments of the powerful stopped exploiting the less fortunate. Allcot might have made the sex workers at the Red Door a decent offer compared to their previous circumstances, but it was still exploitive. He owned other businesses. Why couldn't he let the Red Door employees work for him in another capacity while they went to school and took another path? Because he needed experienced workers so he could be up and running with minimal disruption, that's why.

He wanted a return on his investment as soon as possible. And experienced workers would get him there faster.

"I'm glad you're feeling better," I said as I got up to go. "I'm still willing to check out that healer if you want me to."

She shrugged one shoulder. "Sure. Why not? His name is Talisen Kavanagh. His practice is a few streets over on the corner of Royal and Franklin."

I almost laughed. Two different realities, but it seemed there was some sort of natural order to things that was pretty consistent in both. In my world, Talisen was her husband. There was no need to check him out. Tal was the best of the best. "I know him a little," I lied. "You don't have anything to worry about there."

She smiled again, and this time she seemed to glow with pure happiness. "Well then. Maybe I'll get to know him a little over the next few months and see what comes of his offer."

I was willing to bet that not only would she start working for him but that they'd end up partners sooner rather than later. But I kept that information to myself. She'd find out soon enough.

"I'm going to go help downstairs. I'm glad you're on the mend, Wil." I hugged her, wanting to just feel that connection with my best friend, and was rewarded when she tightened her arms around me.

"You're the best, you know that?" she whispered. "Without you, I'd have never made it this far."

I didn't know what that meant exactly, but I could guess I'd been there emotionally and physically to help her out over the years. "I love you, Wil."

"Love you too, Phoebs."

I released her and swallowed the sudden urge to tell her everything that was going on. It was just that I was used to trusting her and Dax with everything. Holding back in this world was proving to be more difficult than I'd thought it'd be. I turned and reached for the doorknob, but before I could make my escape, Willow said, "Dax is in the storage room rebuilding some shelves today."

"He is?" I asked thickly.

"Eadric ordered him to get it and the kitchen functioning again before Friday."

That fucker. The day we'd come to end Clio's reign as witch overlord, I'd learned the kitchen had been trashed months earlier when Clio had a run-in with another witch. They'd had a knock-down-drag-out fight in the kitchen that ended with appliances blown to pieces and the counters in rubble. "How is he going to do that in just a few days? He's a shifter, not a miracle worker."

Willow shrugged. "No idea, but I bet he could use a hand from someone with some magical ability."

"I guess if the materials can be delivered…," I said, already forming a plan of action.

I was out the door when I heard Willow call, "Be careful!"

If only I had any idea how to do that, I thought as I raced down the stairs and to the back of the house.

Grunts of frustration greeted me from the storage room off to the right of the kitchen. A small smile claimed my lips. I knew those sounds. I heard them often enough when things weren't going Dax's way. I strolled over to the open door and spotted him with his shirt off, a tool belt around his slim hips, his muscles bulging as he tried to install an overhead lighting system. He was using one hand to hold up the track while trying to wield the electric drill with the other.

"Hey, let me help you out," I said, darting inside and climbing up on the small four-foot ladder.

"Phoebe. What are you doing here?"

"Helping." I raised my hands to secure the track. "I've got this."

He just stood there, one hand still securing the light. "You shouldn't be here." He glanced over his shoulder. "Is Allcot back?"

I shook my head. "Still in Baton Rouge as far as I know. Now come on. Let me help. This looks super awkward."

"Right." He finally dropped his arm and then rolled his shoulder as if working out a kink. His dark hair was mussed slightly, and his body glistened with a sheen of sweat.

I had to close my eyes to keep from ogling him. Holy hell, he was gorgeous. Eight-pack abs, well-defined pecs, and broad shoulders that made my fingers itch to touch him. It had been a few weeks since Dax—the other Dax—and I had been together, and it was becoming painfully obvious how much I missed him.

The whirr of the drill whined in my ears as Dax deftly secured the lighting panel. In no time he said, "Done. You can let go now."

I opened my eyes, glanced at his handiwork, and then smiled down at him as I dropped my hands. "You're good at this."

"It's not that difficult." He winked at me and placed the drill on one of the newly installed shelves.

"What else can I do?" I asked, keeping my gaze just over his right shoulder. The man was just too good-looking, and being so close to him had me replaying some X-rated moments I'd shared with his doppelgänger.

"Phoebe," he said, his tone soft.

I cut my gaze to his.

His dark eyes were hooded and a muscle pulsed in his jaw. "I really think you should probably go now."

I let out a huff of irritation and started to climb down the ladder. Only in my haste, my right foot missed the rung and suddenly my world tilted.

"Shit!" he said and quickly grabbed me around the waist, catching me before I fell and cracked my head on something.

My arms went around his neck and the next thing I knew, my feet were on the floor but we were face-to-face, holding each other tight, my slender body pressed up against his muscular one. We stared each other in the eye, and it was as if all the air was sucked out of the room. Everything was still and silent, neither of us breathing.

The weight of his arms around my waist, his scent, that look, all of it was so familiar.

Mine.

The word skittered across my brain. It was what I believed was the natural order of things. That Dax and I belonged together. That given time, we'd likely end up together in this world too. I was caught in the moment, my lips parted as I stared up at him, at the man who was, at his very core, the same one I loved back home.

"Phoebe," he whispered as if he were a tortured man.

"Dax," I whispered back, my voice husky and full of so much emotion I was surprised it didn't crack.

"How am I going to ever let you go?" he asked. And before I could answer, he crushed his lips to mine and kissed me.

Chapter Ten

*D*ax paced the hallway outside Eadric Allcot's Central Business District office. It had been three days since he'd learned who the Mastersons really were. And three days since he'd been forced to cool his jets. Allcot had been out of town and apparently off-grid. Phoebe had been spotted twice more, both times with another shifter of the Masterson pack. But again, Dax had been too late to track her. The only reason he wasn't losing his mind was because he knew she was safe.

The door at the end of the private hallway opened, and Dax strode in, finding Allcot and his consort, Pandora, sitting on a couch in his otherwise cold office. The floor was concrete with a blood-red rug in front of a cream-colored couch and a glass desk, and metal filing cabinets stood at the other end of the room.

"Have a seat, Marrok," Allcot said. He looked the same as he always did, not a day over seventeen and a cocky smile on his too-thin lips. If it weren't for the expensive gray suit, he'd look like the type of kid who'd spent his youth on a skateboard. Pandora had her long blond hair draped over both shoulders, hiding her exaggerated cleavage that was bulging out of her too-tight V-neck tank top.

"Hello, Dax," she said cheerily and sipped red wine from a fancy cut crystal wineglass.

"Good morning, Pandora, Allcot. Thanks for seeing me so soon after getting into town."

"My secretary says you've been a little… impatient," Allcot said, running his fingertips over Pandora's bare arms.

"There's an investigation I'm working on, a homicide, and I came across a sealed case file that I think you'll be able to shed some light on."

His eyebrows rose. "Sealed. Interesting. I'm intrigued."

Pandora chuckled and patted his knee. "Of course you are." She turned her attention to Dax. "What is it?"

He pulled out the sheet and handed it to Allcot. "There was an incident between the Masterson pack and Cryrique that ended in a significant settlement to your company. It came soon after an employee of yours went missing. Do you remember the details?"

Allcot studied the sheet and furrowed his brow. "Who are the Mastersons?"

"They're a shifter pack. The leader lives in Lakeview, but they have members in Uptown and Lakeshore. Seems to be a conscientious, upstanding group that's working to build up the less fortunate in the city."

"I don't recall any settlement," Allcot said. "I'm sorry, Marrok. One of my managers must have handled this. I can have one of them look into it, but we process a lot of settlements. It might take a bit to find it."

Dax sucked in a sharp breath. He should've known Allcot didn't even remember details of major settlements. The vampire was so rich, whatever the amount was it had probably been pocket change. "All right," he said, trying to conceal his frustration. "If you could have your legal department look into it and call me as soon as possible, that would be great. I suspect Phoebe's out in the field working on this and—"

"I remember this," Pandora said, her expression turning from mildly curious to downright furious. "Eadric, it's the pack that was hunting witches and tried to go after my sister Nicola."

"What?" Dax asked, startled. "They tried to kill Nicola? She must've been a young girl then."

"She was." Pandora stood. "You know why there aren't a ton of witches in this town?" She nodded toward the piece of paper I'd brought. "Because ten years ago that pack hunted witches. They think witchcraft is some dark evil. It's part of their weird religion."

And Phoebe was caught up in something to do with them? He couldn't help but wonder when or why. There wasn't a directive from Halston. If there was, Dax would've known. And why hadn't Phoebe contacted him about it? Was she still shaken up after he'd been captured by King and almost turned into a supershifter? That didn't make sense.

"What happened? I'd have thought you would've had Eadric's vampires tear them all limb from limb," Dax said.

"Oh, they did." She gave Allcot a soft smile. "Not all of them, but the ones who were the designated hunters."

"And the settlement?" Dax asked. "Did the Void prosecute anyone?"

"The ones who actually murdered the witches were already dead. So the Void stayed out of it at that point, but Eadric sued them on my behalf so their resources would be depleted. But we ended up not taking money; instead, we made them sign a document that stated they would change all their teaching on witches and curb their hate speech—otherwise, we'd bankrupt them. They went for it, and ever since then, they've been acting like model citizens. Because if they don't, Eadric will take them to the cleaners on Nicola's behalf."

Dax let out a low whistle. It didn't pay to piss off the powerful leader of Cryrique. He'd already known that of course, but he hadn't been prepared for a settlement agreement that basically forced an entire pack to behave in a socially acceptable manner. "That's... interesting."

"You said Phoebe is investigating them now?" Pandora asked. Fire burned in her bright blue eyes. "Did another witch go missing?"

Dax shook his head. "No. Not as far as I know. One of their shifters died. Looks like a witch did it with a death spell."

Pandora blinked and then sank back down into the couch. Eadric wrapped his arm around her and pulled her against his side. She tapped her fingers against his chest. "Looks like someone wants revenge."

"You think that's what it is?" That made a hell of a lot more sense than any theory he'd come up with. Unless... what if they'd started to target witches again? Maybe ones from surrounding areas that wouldn't be on the radar in New Orleans.

"It's a possibility. But what do I know?" Pandora leaned forward and stared him in the eye. "No matter how upstanding those shifters appear, they are intolerant and dangerous. If Phoebe's investigating them, she's in danger."

That's exactly what Dax had been afraid of. He nodded.

"I think you're right. And that means I need to find her sooner rather than later."

"Do you have any leads?" Pandora asked.

Dax's phone buzzed. He held up a finger and glanced at the text. His heart leaped. Finally, Phoebe had used her credit card. "Just got one. Gotta go. Thank you, Pandora. You've been very helpful."

"Let me know if you need my help," Pandora said.

He was already walking out the door when he called over his shoulder, "I will."

Dax sped through the streets of New Orleans, ignoring posted speed limits and swerving to avoid the never-ending potholes. This was the first time he'd gotten a hit on her credit card since he'd called in the order.

The card had been used in Uptown on Freret Street at a store called Pixie Dust. He knew the place well. They stocked ingredients for spells and even rented out work space for witches to concoct their spells somewhere other than their own kitchen.

He knew the chances of Phoebe still being there when he arrived were slim, but he could at the very least interview the staff. He could find out what she'd bought and make an educated guess on what she'd use it for. It was also possible she'd mentioned where she was headed or some other seemingly random fact that might help him track her down.

The store was squeezed between a microbrew pub and a sushi place in the up-and-coming neighborhood. Dax parked across the street, quickly sent Leo a text to let him know he was following a lead, and then hopped out.

The front window was stocked with how-to books, silver jewelry, and a display of dried herbs. Inside, the place smelled of a strange mix of lavender and sandalwood.

The witch behind the counter looked up from her magazine and wrinkled her nose at him. "We don't carry anything for shifters."

Charming, he thought. "I'm not here to buy anything. I'm looking for someone."

Her lips formed a thin, tight line. "Madeline isn't here."

He had no idea who Madeline was, nor did he care. Dax flipped open his wallet and pulled out the picture of Phoebe he'd been carrying around for the past few days. "I'm looking for this witch. I have reason to believe she was here about twenty minutes ago."

The cashier eyed the photo, and Dax saw the recognition dawn in her gaze just before she looked up at him, her expression bored. "Never seen her before."

He let out a small snort of derision. "Are you sure about that?" With his other hand, he reached into his pocket and pulled out his Arcane ID. "If you're not truthful, I'll have reason to believe you're hiding something and a whole host of agents will come raining down on this little shop of yours. A thorough search would likely be a huge hassle even if we don't find any illegal substances."

"That's fucked up, man."

He shrugged. "Maybe, but if you've seen this woman and are holding back due to some solidarity code or just because you plain don't like shifters, then you're impeding an investigation, and as far as I'm concerned, you get what you deserve." It was a shitty way to get what he wanted, but he was tired of wasting time.

"Fine. Fuck. Chill out," she said, throwing her hands in the air. "Yeah, I saw her. She was here buying some candles and a silver pendant."

"Is that all?" he demanded, glancing at the herbs in the bin behind her.

"No." She tapped a button on her register. "Looks like she went for some wolfsbane and silver flakes." Her lips curved into a shitty little smile. "Looks like your girl doesn't like shifters too much, doesn't it?"

"Looks like it. Which way did she go?"

She shook her head. "No idea."

"You didn't see her get in her car? A gray Charger?"

The cashier's eyes lit up. "Gods, I love that car. It's a beauty. I drool over it every morning."

"She's been here before?" Dax asked, surprised.

"Yep. A couple of days ago. Parked right in front. I spent most of the time admiring that piece of machinery. I've always wanted a muscle car."

"Right." He glanced around once more. "You said she drives by every day. Where do you think she goes?"

"The River Roux. It's the café on the corner. I think she eats half her meals there."

Jackpot. That was the break Dax needed. He knocked his knuckles on the counter. "Thank you. You've been very helpful."

"Whatever, dude. Just don't go all Sheriff Crankypants on me again. It harshes my chill."

"Looks like you're safe," Dax said and hurried outside. The first thing he did was walk over to the River Roux, the café on the corner of the block. It was a breakfast and lunch place that appeared to be ramping up for the lunch service. He stepped inside and scanned the tables. There was no one who looked like Phoebe, but that didn't appease him. He knew better than anyone how good she was at disguises. He needed a minute to really assess each patron.

Instead of getting a table, he took a seat at the end of the bar, giving him a decent view of the restaurant. A waitress hurried over and took his order for a sweet tea. After carefully scanning the faces of all the patrons, he was satisfied none of them were Phoebe. And when the waitress returned, he handed her a couple of bills and left with his to-go cup.

But he wasn't in the least bit discouraged. If Phoebe had walked to the store, that meant she was likely staying somewhere nearby. He just couldn't place where that might be. There weren't a lot of hotels in the area. Maybe she was making use of a short-term rental. He climbed back into the Trooper and was just getting ready to pull away from the curb when a gunmetal-gray car shot past him.

"There you are," he said and stepped on the gas, cutting in front of a blue Toyota. The Toyota swerved, and Dax thought he heard the high-pitched sound of the horn, but he didn't care. Phoebe's car was turning left onto one of the residential streets.

He sped up and followed. He made the turn just in time to see the Charger slip into a garage at the end of the block.

"Gotcha," he said and then turned right onto another street and parked a few blocks away, not wanting his Trooper to be visible near her safe house, just in case someone recognized it.

By the time he made it back to the house on the corner, his entire body was damp from the oppressive humidity and he was a little cranky that he'd had to track down his partner, but he sucked in a deep breath and told himself to chill. Phoebe wouldn't be doing this if she didn't have a good reason.

As Dax walked up to the front door, it was clear to him that the house was one of Phoebe's safe houses. He recognized the lights that were outfitted with microphones and cameras that lined the walkway. The run-down landscaping and the peeling paint was familiar too. She didn't want any of her safe houses to stand out and preferred ones that looked like they needed a serious update. No one would ever suspect that on the inside, the house was outfitted with state-of-the-art security equipment and computer systems.

But Dax knew, and he did his best to stay out of view of the cameras by walking on the overgrown lawn. It wasn't until he jumped over to the front porch that he knew he could be seen on the monitors inside.

Surely she'd let him in, wouldn't she? He pressed the doorbell and stood right in front of the camera lens. "Come on, Phoebe. I don't know what's going on, but you've got me worried. Open the door."

There was no sound, no hint of movement on the inside. To anyone else, the house would seem empty, deserted maybe. But he was certain she was in there. He knocked, and when that went unanswered, he pressed his left hand to the door and grabbed the knob with his right. Then he said his name. "Dax Alton Marrok."

The lock clicked and the door magically opened. He let out a sigh of relief. Phoebe had spelled the other houses so that he could gain entry if he needed to. But he'd never known if she'd spelled all of them. Why would she if he didn't even know where they were? Thank the gods for her thoroughness.

He took two steps into the house and then froze.

Phoebe was standing in the foyer, a dagger in one hand and an agate glowing in the other. He recognized the agate right away. It was her sunshine spell, meant to knock out vampires. It wouldn't hurt him, at least not permanently. But the dagger...

"Whoa. No need for that, Phoebs," he said, raising his hands in a stop motion. "I'm here to help."

She stood there, frozen for a few beats. Then the light in the agate blinked out and the dagger fell to the ground. Phoebe leaped forward and crushed him in a hug.

His arms went around her automatically, holding her against him. She felt the same, hard and soft at the same time. And her skin smelled like sunshine, just like it always did, but something was different. And he couldn't quite put his finger on it.

"I can't believe you're here," she said into his neck, her voice cracking a little as she choked on a tiny sob.

"Phoebe, what's wrong? What happened?"

She pulled back, her sad black eyes swimming with tears. "I know what happened to my brother. A pack killed him, and now they're after me."

Chapter Eleven

*D*ax's arms encircled me, holding me tight as if he were never going to let me go. And if I was honest, I could have stayed right there in his arms forever. His woodsy scent and his faint citrus taste were exactly what I expected when I was in the arms of Dax Marrok. He might be from a different universe, but he was still *Dax* in all the ways that mattered.

"Whoa," Dax said as he broke away from me. His dark eyes were full of lust as he stared at me.

I smiled. "Thanks for stepping in there. I guess I really could've hurt myself."

His lips curved into a sexy little smile, and I was just contemplating kissing him again when I heard the faint sound of footsteps.

We both sprang apart. I pressed my fingertips to my lips while Dax grabbed his shirt from a nearby shelf and pulled it over his head, hiding those glorious muscles. He wasn't quite as built as my Dax back home, but that was because my Dax had been drugged not too long ago with a substance that was meant to turn him into a supershifter. But this Dax was close. It seemed like he did more physical labor than his counterpart.

We were both silent as we listened to the footsteps fade into the background. Whoever it was had retreated.

"That can't happen again," Dax said, turning his back to me.

I knew he was right. If Allcot found out... the consequences were unthinkable. Not to mention, I wasn't the Phoebe he'd known all his life. Was it considered cheating to be with this Dax in this world while I was in a relationship with the other one? I didn't know. All I knew is that it was too dangerous for me to be playing this game. "You're right. It won't."

Dax hung his head and ran a hand through his hair. Then he blew out a breath and silently walked out of the storage room.

I followed him into the kitchen. "Where do you want me?"

He spun around, gaping at me. "What?"

"Where do you want me?" I asked again, waving a hand around at the messy kitchen. "I can help you move appliances out or start cleaning up debris."

"Oh. Right." He glanced down at his feet and shook his head.

"What is it, Dax? Do you not want my help?" I grinned at him. He'd completely misunderstood me, and I don't know why, but it amused me to no end.

"It's not that..." He shook his head and tried again. "If you won't take no for an answer, then I guess you can start bagging up the debris. I've got the appliances covered."

I saluted him. "I'm on it, boss."

Chuckling to himself, he walked outside while I grabbed a couple of large garbage bags and got to work.

Three hours later, we were sitting in the courtyard under the oak tree, eating sandwiches and drinking tea.

"You worked hard," Dax said.

I jerked my head up and gave him a weird look. "I've always been a hard worker."

He snorted. "No you haven't."

"Yes I have," I insisted. As a teenager, I'd always worked an after-school job, and then when I was training for the Void as a vampire hunter, I worked security for a couple of different clubs. But this Dax wouldn't know that. I started to wonder what kind of life my counterpart might've had in this world.

"You can't call sitting around your mom's dance studio all day actual work. All you did was answer the phones and sign people in." He picked up his drink and took a long sip.

I stared at him, my mouth open as I took in his words. My counterpart had a mom in this world?

"Why are you looking at me like that?" he asked, frowning. "You're not seriously upset that I called you out on that lie, are you?"

I started to ask about her but then shut my mouth and shook my head. I was intensely curious about what happened to her and my dad, but I'd have to wait for Seth to return to find out. "No. I guess not."

"Hey, Phoebs, I was just messing with you." His tone was apologetic, then turned to one of sympathy. "I know you miss her."

I squeezed my eyes shut and tried to recall my mom. She'd been elegant, full of life, and the most talented witch in all of New Orleans. But the thing I loved most about her was her joy. She'd loved me and Seth and never failed to shower us with kisses and hugs. I could almost feel her scooping me up into one of her mama-bear hugs, and I wrapped my arms around myself as if to keep the memory alive. She died when I was far too young, and my recollection of her was starting to become hazy.

"Hey," Dax said softly, his big hand resting gently on my bare knee. "What are you thinking about?"

My eyes popped open. "Her hugs. She was really great at them."

"You're right about that." His fingers pressed into my flesh as he gave me a little squeeze. "I miss her too, you know."

It was so strange to be sitting with this man, discussing my mother. But the idea that this Dax loved her too filled me with such joy and contentment I couldn't help smiling at him. "I'm sure she loved the hell out of you."

"Of course she did. Once she even told me I was her favorite." He winked at me. "It was right after Seth ruined one of her spells by spilling sea salt into the herb mixture."

I chuckled. "He's always been a bit of a klutz in the spell-casting department."

Dax went on to regale me with a few stories of good intentions gone awry when it came to my brother, and it didn't take long to figure out that the pair had been best friends growing up. And I started to wonder if he knew that Seth wasn't the same boy he'd once known and loved.

I put my sandwich down, no longer hungry. "Can I ask you a question?"

"Of course you can." He turned to me, giving me his full attention.

"Are you and Seth still close? I mean, do you two—"

"No." The answer was instantaneous. "Seth and I… that ended years ago. You know that."

What ended exactly? Their friendship? "Why?"

His fist curled and anger flashed in those gorgeous eyes of his. "Oh, I don't know. Maybe it has something to do with being betrayed and left to rot in a whorehouse for over eight years."

"What are you talking about?" I asked before I could censor myself.

He gave me a strange look and put the rest of his sandwich down. "Are you seriously telling me you don't know how I ended up here?"

"Yes," I said, because it was the truth. And I really wanted to know. This man was so strong, so capable, it was hard to imagine how he'd entered an agreement with Clio unless he was forced somehow.

"I did it to keep an eye on you," he said so softly that I barely heard him.

My breath whooshed out of my lungs. "But… why?"

"What do you mean, why? Don't be so dense." He scoffed and stood, his anger apparent in his jerky movements as he paced in front of me. "When your mother died and Clio took you as payment for her debts, your brother and I decided it would be me who'd come and keep an eye on you. He said he was working on a plan to purchase our freedom. He said he just needed a few weeks."

Dread settled in my belly, and I wanted to tell him to stop. That I didn't want to hear what happened, but I had to know.

Dax let out a humorless snort. "But then four years went by before he showed up here with Allcot to take you back to his plantation. Imagine my surprise when the bastard didn't even try to do anything to help me to get away from Clio. We were best friends. I watched over you for four fucking years, keeping you safe from the worst this city had to offer. And what did I get? Nothing. Not even a 'Sorry, Dax.'"

Eight years ago. Eight years ago was when my own brother went missing. When he'd crossed over. Had he known about the deal Dax and his doppelgänger made? I doubted it. He'd been flying blind. It probably took him years to get to a place where he could affect any change.

"So lucky me." Dax continued on his rant. "I've been here, indentured to Clio, because that bitch can't just give a person a job. No, she needed control, and I had to sign a magical contract just for the privilege of working in this shithole. And it's all because eight years ago I loved you too much to let you rot here. I thought for sure you'd try to do something to break her spell once you were free, but I'm betting Allcot wouldn't let you. He doesn't like the competition. And it appears the only reason Clio is gone is because your old friend Willow got tangled up with that witch when she ended up owing her too much. Isn't it funny how only three months after she checked into the Red Door, your husband and his band of vamp assholes tore this place to shreds?"

"And you're still indentured," I finished for him.

"That's right." He pierced me with his dark eyes. "And now here you are, delighting me with your presence, and I know that if Allcot finds out, he'll either kill me or torture me. Yet I don't seem to care because I'm enjoying the hell out of visiting with the girl I fell in love with when I was fifteen years old. Do me a favor, will you?"

"Anything," I said instantly, still stunned by the revelation of his life.

"Go back into the club and leave me the hell alone."

Our gazes locked, and I saw all the pain that loving my doppelgänger had caused him. He was torn up inside, doing his best to hold it together. But in that moment, I knew if I didn't find a way to free him, he'd be broken and there'd be no saving him. Eight years was a long time to be someone's servant, but serving the man who was married to the woman he so clearly loved would be worse than torture. I wouldn't let him endure it.

"Listen, Dax—"

"Just go, Phoebe," he said softly. "It's better for both of us."

The barely concealed pain in his voice made me nod and silently go back into the club.

Chapter Twelve

"*T*he pack killed your brother?" Dax asked Phoebe, shock rooting his feet to the floor. "When?"

She didn't answer as she retreated back into the house. It was a small cottage, but the inside was freshly painted and well-kept. "How did you find me?"

"Good tracking skills," he said and wrapped his arms around her.

She stiffened, pressing her hands to his chest. "What are you doing?"

"Hugging you." He glanced down at her, frowned, and released her. She clearly didn't want his embrace. "Sorry. I thought after your brother and… never mind." Dax didn't know what to say. She was… different. Cold and closed off. "Are you all right?"

She shook her head. "I told you they killed my brother and are trying to kill me."

"Right." Dax walked into the small kitchen and poured himself a glass of water. He took a seat at the kitchen counter and eyed her. "Is there a reason you didn't call me? I've been really worried, Phoebe."

"I…" She shook her head, and a tear rolled down her cheek.

"Shit." He got up and wrapped his arms around her again. Phoebe wasn't a crier. "I'm sorry. I shouldn't have led with that. It's all right. Tell me about your brother. How did you find out?"

Her arms came around him, and for the first time in days, he felt whole again. When had he started feeling like half a person without her? He had no idea.

"The other night when they came after me. They showed me pictures, told me he was dead and it was my turn. So I…" She choked on a sob and buried her head against his chest.

They? Not just Maci? "Do you know who they are?"

She shook her head. "I didn't recognize them. But… the girl, I…" Her voice trailed off and she looked a little panicked.

"It was self-defense." Relief rushed through him as he said the words, and he hugged her tighter. "It's okay. You did what you had to do. I just don't know why you're out here on your own. You know I would've been here to help you track them down."

She blinked up at him, her black eyes bright with unshed tears. "I just… can we deal with all that later?"

Damn. He was an asshole. Dax just wasn't used to his partner falling apart right before his eyes. But she had just learned her brother was dead. Of course she was going to be messed up. She'd spent the past few months searching for him after finding out he was alive, and now she'd lost him again. "Sure, Phoebs. Anything you need. Let's work on bringing these shifters in, and then we can deal with all of that later."

She nodded and pulled out of his embrace. "Have you heard of the Masterson pack?"

"I hadn't up until a few days ago. But I've been doing my homework and learned a little about them. How about you?"

"Do you know where to find them?" she asked, narrowing her eyes.

"Some of them." Dax took another step back, unsettled. She was acting really strange. "Why don't you fill me in on what exactly happened the day you left the infirmary so I can get an idea of what's going on."

She glanced away and ran a hand through her dark hair. "You mean the day Maci Masterson attacked me?"

"Yes." Dax sat back down on the kitchen stool and waited.

"Well, I'd been in the infirmary, right?" She said it as if she were asking Dax to confirm, so he nodded. "Right. Anyway, I wanted to stretch my legs. It was getting dark out, but I figured if I walked around the Garden District, it would be fine. But then she just came out of nowhere. We struggled, and in the end I had no choice. It was either me or her."

"I figured it had come down to that," Dax said with a nod even though his gut told him something was seriously off. That wasn't how Phoebe reported her interactions. Again, he reminded himself that she'd just learned of her brother's death. It was entirely possible she was just in shock and not acting herself. "What happened after that? You didn't call or report it to the Void office."

"I just… I don't know." She shook her head and stared straight ahead. "I just needed time to process, I guess."

"And to absorb the news of your brother?"

She blew out a breath and nodded as if relieved. "Yes. I haven't exactly been myself."

"I kind of noticed," he said gently.

"Right. Well…" She pulled a piece of paper from her pocket and handed it to him. Then she backed up, putting distance between them. "Can you work on finding these members of the pack? They're the ones involved with Seth's death."

"Sure, but—"

"I need to shower," she said and took off into the bedroom, closing the door behind her.

Dax stood there, stunned. That hadn't been the reunion he'd imagined. The pipes groaned and he heard the rush of water as he moved to the couch and studied the paper she'd given him. It had a list of four names.

~~Maci Masterson~~

Gerry Coster

Prim Masterson

Lincoln Frost

It took him a phone call to the Void and less than five minutes to get the background information on her targets. They were all cousins of Maci Masterson. They all worked in the city. None of them had a record. As far as he could tell, they'd put the pack trouble behind them years ago. But what about the attacks on Phoebe and her brother? Why now?

An ache started to form above his eyes, and he pressed two fingers to his forehead, trying to ease the pressure. He downloaded the background reports of the four cousins from an email and scanned the sheets. After making no real connections, he started to make notes to see if a pattern would emerge.

Names, family, known associates, employment, addresses.

None of them worked together. They ran in different social circles. They weren't even associated with any of the major paranormal players in the city like Allcot or the new shifter pack that had disbanded a few months ago. They had family in common, but that was about it. They didn't even live near each other.

There had to be something. Prior to this week, he certainly hadn't known anything about the Masterson pack. He couldn't imagine Phoebe had either. Had she stumbled on something while she'd been looking for her brother? If so, why hadn't she said anything?

His brain was whirling, and none of it made sense. He dropped the papers and got up to pace. Sometimes movement helped. Dax glanced at the clock. Phoebe had been in the bathroom for at least thirty minutes. He started to worry again and wondered if he should check on her. He turned his attention back to the papers and listened to the sound of the clock ticking on the wall.

After a while, he lost his battle to leave her alone, and he reached for the bedroom doorknob and found it was locked. "What the fuck?" Since when did Phoebe feel the need to lock him out?

There was no denying it. Phoebe wasn't herself. She was either spelled or suffering some sort of mental break about her brother. He needed to know one way or another.

"Phoebe?" He knocked on the door, but the water was still running. How long had it been? Forty-five minutes? An hour? Far too long. He knocked once more, and when she didn't respond, he dug into his pocket and pulled out his trusty lockpick set. In less than thirty seconds, the door popped open.

The room was dark, but there was a light under the bathroom door. He knocked once. "Phoebs? It's me—I'm coming in."

Again, no response.

Steeling himself for what he might find, he pushed the door open and scanned the empty bathroom. "Fuck!"

He turned off the water, then rushed over to the open window and peeked out. Phoebe was long gone. His footsteps were loud on the old hardwood as he ran through the small house and outside, scanning the area for her. He wasn't surprised to see the garage door open and her car gone. She'd completely made a run for it.

Why? That was the million-dollar question. An ache formed in his gut. As far as he could tell, there was only one explanation. She was responsible for Maci's death and had decided to go on the run... even from him. He walked slowly back into the house, his head down, almost unable to process what had happened.

He'd been covering for her for days, and she'd taken off as if he was the enemy. Her betrayal was more than a flesh wound. It cut deep, and it made him question everything he thought he knew about his partner. With his jaw set in determination, he strode back into the house and started to search for answers.

The place was stocked with necessities. The cupboards had canned food, packages of pasta and rice, canned milk, and other nonperishable provisions. There were also take-out containers in the refrigerator. It was obvious she hadn't been grocery shopping. Dax moved from the kitchen into the bedroom. And that's when he hit pay dirt.

The duffel bag that was always in her Charger was sitting on the floor of the closet. Its contents of wigs and a variety of outfits that would allow her to pass as a tourist, a student, or even a businesswoman were tossed all over the place as if she'd been frantically searching for something. It was the bag she kept on her at all times for various emergency situations when she was in the field. Only she didn't have it now, which would make finding her easier. He couldn't help but wonder why she hadn't taken it with her.

Dax gathered the clothes and shoved them back into the bag and grabbed the handles. He wasn't leaving it there. If she came back and got the disguises, it would only make it harder for him to find her.

Fuming, he hefted the bag and was ready to storm out of the house when he spotted a notebook that had been underneath the bag. He crouched and recognized it immediately. It was Phoebe's journal, the one she used for important information she didn't want to forget, like spells she was working on or suspects in her various cases.

He picked it up and flipped through it. A small, ripped piece of paper fell out. It had the address to the safe house scrawled across it in shaky handwriting. Frowning with confusion, he stuffed the paper back into the journal, tossed it into the bag, and strode out of the safe house, trying to ignore the ache in the middle of his chest.

The woman he loved had just gone rogue.

Chapter Thirteen

"What's going on up here?" Pandora poked her head into my herb studio. "I thought you were going to come help with dinner?"

I'd just flopped down in my chair after checking for the third time for any herb or root that was used for breaking curses. There wasn't one vial of bloodroot, nettles, pokeroot, or any of the other herbs I was accustomed to working with. "I was just trying to brew a new potion. Sorry." I stood and walked over to her. "Are they back yet?"

"Yep. Just arrived twenty minutes ago. Eadric is asking for you." She glanced over at my workstation. "What kind of potion?"

"Oh, you know, the usual. The kind for attracting good fortune." It wasn't a total lie. If I did manage to brew up something that would break Dax's curse, it would be great fortune for him.

"Don't you usually work more with agates?"

"Usually," I said, careful to keep my tone light. "I was just trying something new." I jerked my head toward the door. "Ready? I'll help you finish up dinner."

"Phoebe," she started and glanced over her shoulder at my workstation. "You're not working on anything you shouldn't be, right?"

I wanted to scream at her. How could she live in this world and act like everything was fine? Maybe because her life seemed perfect. Allcot didn't control her. She seemed happy with Seth and her child. Was it really that easy to just turn a blind eye? It wasn't worth fighting about though. I had a plan, and with any luck, I was going to free Dax of his curse to work for Allcot and find a way back to my own reality. "It's nothing to worry about, Pandora. It's a harmless potion. Come on."

Garlic and basil wafted up the stairs, hitting my senses as I sailed out of my studio. "What did you make? Lasagna?"

"Yes." She smiled, joy lighting her blue eyes. "You know it's Seth's favorite. I wanted something special to welcome him home."

I did know. Seth had always been partial to Italian food. A tingle of happiness skated through my heart. Even though I was stuck in this strange reality, it was nice to be able to share in these simple pleasures again with my brother and his family. "It smells wonderful. Thank you. I should've helped."

"It was nothing. I was happy to do it," she said, following me down the stairs.

I guessed it was good that she was happy to do it. But frankly, it ticked me off that she was the only one who seemed to be in charge of the domestic tasks in Allcot's plantation home. The women in this world were treated as property, and I wanted no part in perpetuating that gross gender role. If I had my way, the men would each take on a night of cooking, while the women hung out in the office and discussed something more interesting that cooking temperatures. We strolled into the kitchen, and Pandora immediately made a beeline for her lasagna that was resting on the counter. I headed for the wine. Lots of it.

Once I had the table set, Pandora called the men. Allcot and Seth emerged from Allcot's office, their heads bent together in discussion. Whatever they were talking about, they were too engrossed to notice me. Or so I thought.

"Phoebe, what the hell are you wearing?" Allcot snapped.

I glanced down at my jeans and the T-shirt I'd fished out of Seth's wardrobe. My closet was full of June Cleaver dresses that I'd rather burn than wear again. "What does it look like I'm wearing?"

Seth cringed at my tone, but I kept my shoulders straight and didn't back down.

"Go upstairs and change," Allcot ordered. "That isn't appropriate dinner attire."

I glanced around and let out a chuckle. "For who? Are we having a dinner party no one told us about?"

"For me," Allcot said, his voice low but commanding. It was clear he didn't like to be challenged in front of Seth.

Well, too fucking bad. "I think I look fine."

He started to walk toward me, but Seth cut him off and got to me first. "Excuse us for a second," Seth said. "I need a word with my sister."

Normally I would've balked about being manhandled by my brother, but the fact was, I wanted a private moment with him too. So I let him lead me all the way upstairs and back to my studio that doubled as my bedroom.

"What are you doing? Are you trying to rock the boat?" he asked, his voice wary.

"Maybe," I said, placing my hands on my hips. "I thought you were going to go back home and find you know who? Where have you been for the past four days?"

"With Allcot. You know that," he said, walking over to the small closet. I'd moved some clothes into the room just so I wouldn't have to run into Allcot every morning while getting dressed. Seth pulled out the one decent dress in my closet. "Put this on. He likes this one."

"Of course he does. The V goes almost to my belly button," I said dryly.

"It doesn't go that far. If it did, Allcot would never let you wear it."

I rolled my eyes. It showed off plenty, but whatever. This was a sexy dress and wasn't worth arguing over. But if someone tried to make me wear polka dots and saddle shoes, I was going to snap. I took the dress from him and said, "Turn around."

My brother did as I said and I got to work on changing.

"Now, what were you doing in Baton Rouge?" I asked again.

"Some research on another pleasure club," he finally said. "It's a similar situation to the Red Door. A few women got caught up in the wrong mess and I asked Allcot to see if we can add it to the company portfolio."

I narrowed my eyes at him, knowing instantly that there was more to the story. "Why that club? Don't they all have ethics problems?"

"Probably." He stared at his feet, and for a second I was convinced he wasn't going to tell me the whole truth. But then he blurted, "I found Heather. She's working there."

"Heather Welsh?" I asked, astonished.

He nodded, not saying anything.

"I thought she passed away in a car accident years ago... or did you mean her doppelgänger works there?"

"Not her doppelgänger," he said quietly. Then he moved so close to me he was clutching my arm tightly. "My Heather did not die. She ended up here somehow, and it's why I crossed over in the first place."

I let out a small gasp. Heather Welsh had been his girlfriend when he'd been training at the Void. But then disaster struck. Or at least I thought it had. "She's *here?*"

"Yeah and... I asked Allcot to get her out." His expression was pained, and I wondered if it was because the love of his life was tied to a whorehouse or because he'd still been searching for her while married to Pandora. Probably both.

"Is he going to do it?" I asked, more than a little curious.

"Yes." He sucked in a breath. "But he did say that if I ever hurt Pandora, he'll rip my head off, so there's that."

Of course he had. Even in this universe it was easy to see that Allcot had feelings for her. It was all in the way he looked at her. There was a wistfulness that didn't exist when he looked at me... thank the gods. I didn't want him anywhere near me. "I'm not sure what to make of that, big brother," I said, worry for him pushing out my annoyance. "Is that going to be hard to deal with? You have Pandora now."

He just shrugged. "Does it matter? I can't leave her there either way."

That was my brother—the one who always had to save everyone. "Can I ask you something?"

He gave me a weary look. "Yeah, I guess."

"Why did it take you so long to rescue my doppelgänger from the Red Door?"

He took a seat on a trunk near my closet and ran a hand

through his thick dark hair. "You have no idea what it was like for me when I got here. There were enemies, debts, lies. You name it, I had to navigate it. And all I wanted to do was find Heather. But she was long gone, and I…" He gave me a little shake of his head. "Pandora came along. She helped me navigate a shit ton of bad situations, and we ended up together with Lex on the way. It took me a long time to get to a place where I could help, Phoebs. Then I went to work for Allcot, and he was the first chance I had to do anything."

"She doesn't love him, does she?" I asked, just to fulfill my own curiosity.

"I think she wanted to, but she's in love with Dax and Allcot will never set him free. Because of that, she hates him." He held his hands palms up. "I did the best I could. I know it wasn't enough."

I believed him. He wouldn't want me working in such a place, and it would be hard to watch my doppelgänger there. "Did you know your counterpart promised Dax he'd find a way to release him from Clio?"

"Yeah. He said something about it once. More like sneered at me. But I swear to God, there has been nothing I could do while also keeping Pandora and Lex safe."

I patted his arm. "I know. You're a good guy."

"I'm not sure about that." He stared over my shoulder, lost in his own thoughts.

I cleared my throat. "Seth?"

"Yeah?"

"You still need to go back to our world. Bring the other Phoebe here so I can go home." That pained look came over his face again, but I wasn't having it. "I'm not kidding. I can't stay here. I don't belong here. If you don't do this for me, I'll find a way to get back there. A curse, a hex, a potion, a summoning. Hell, I don't know, but I'll visit every voodoo practitioner, shaman, and witch in this state until I get what I need."

He blanched. "No! You can't do that. It's too fucking dangerous, Phoebs. Promise me you won't even try."

I shook my head. "Forget it. You promised me you'd go get the other Phoebe."

A muscle pulsed in his jaw, but finally he gave me a curt nod. "Fine. I'll leave first thing in the morning."

"Not after dinner?" I pressed.

"No. I need a night with Pandora and my son."

It was then I saw the anxiousness in his expression. "Is it dangerous for you to hop worlds?"

"Always," he admitted. "I'm dead in that world, remember? When I just pop up out of nowhere, people start to ask questions."

I winced, knowing my tenacity to find him hadn't helped him any in that regard. "Sorry, big brother. You should've just told me what was going on."

"I was trying to protect you." He gave me a gentle smile.

"And I was trying to rescue you." I chuckled. "We make some pair, don't we?"

"We sure do." He got up from his spot and pulled me into a bear hug that only Seth could deliver. "I love you, Phoebs. And I've missed the hell out of you."

"I love you too," I said, sniffing back tears.

"Be careful while I'm gone, all right? You might be married to Allcot, but he's still dangerous."

"I've never been afraid of that over-cocky vampire," I said.

"Maybe not. But he's just as big of an ass in this reality as he is in ours. Maybe more so. He has less to lose."

That was the cold hard truth. In our reality he had a major corporation and had unprecedented influence over the city of New Orleans. He also had Pandora. In this one, he had a pain-in-the-ass wife and an organization that got the job done, but it wasn't a multibillion-dollar company either. "I see what you mean."

"Good. Now let's eat before Pandora chews us both out."

I looked down at my dress and smoothed the material. It was far too fancy for a lasagna dinner, but when we reached the dining room, Allcot's eyes lit up with approval and his shitty demeanor vanished.

Score one for the exposed cleavage.

Chapter Fourteen

*L*ight shone from the long front windows of the Greek Revival house Phoebe shared with Willow and Talisen. Dax pulled his Trooper to a stop out front and blew out a long breath. How was he going to tell Phoebe's best friend that he suspected Phoebe was the witch he was looking for?

The front door opened, and Willow poked her head out. "Dax? Is that you?"

It was time to face the music. He hauled himself out of the vehicle and gave her a small wave.

"Any news?"

He nodded, and when he reached her he frowned. "It's not good news."

"Oh goddess," Willow said, pressing her hand to her throat. "Is she... all right? Tell me she's all right, Dax."

"She's not hurt, as far as I know anyway." The physical pain in his chest made it difficult to breathe. "Listen, can I come in? We need to talk."

"Of course." She stepped back and opened the door wide

for him. Her wolf, Link, was in his cute shih tzu form and came running up, yapping away.

"It's me, Link," Dax said, kneeling down to pet the gold-and-white pup. He wiggled his body, excitement taking over as he jumped up on Dax, giving him a big wet kiss on the cheek.

"He's happy to see you," Willow said with a smile.

At least someone is, he thought. He patted Link on the head and stood, jamming his hands in his pockets. "I saw Phoebe today."

"That's good," she said but sounded cautious. "Where has she been?"

"At one of her safe houses."

Footsteps sounded on the stairs, and Dax glanced up, finding Willow's husband Talisen.

"Dax, hey man. Good to see you."

"You too," Dax said with a nod and watched as he kissed Willow on the cheek. The pair just radiated love. Both of them practically glowed when they gazed at each other, and Dax felt a sudden pang of jealousy he'd never experienced before. Where the hell had that come from? He chided himself, but he already knew. He wanted that with Phoebe, had secretly thought they were on that path, but now... He shook his head.

"What's wrong, Dax?" Willow asked, her blue eyes full of concern. "You look like you're ready to come right out of your skin."

He felt like it too. "Sorry. It's been a long day."

"Let's go upstairs to the kitchen. I think I've got just the thing you need." She crooked a finger, beckoning both men to follow her.

"After you," Talisen said.

Dax's limbs were heavy as he hauled himself up to the second floor. This wasn't the conversation he wanted to be having. All he wanted was his partner back, the sane, kick-ass woman who didn't take shit from anyone but had a heart of gold. The one he'd been with earlier in the day had been a stranger.

"We had a visitor today," Willow said as she pulled three bottles out of her refrigerator and placed them on the table.

Dax took a seat and raised an eyebrow. "Was Phoebe here?"

"No, unfortunately." She walked back into the kitchen and opened her cookie jar. After arranging some on the plate, she returned to the table and placed them in front of Dax. "Her brother Seth showed up looking for her."

"What?" Dax felt the blood drain from his face. "That's not possible, is it?"

"Why not?" Talisen asked, opening his bottle of Mocha in Motion. It was a mocha-flavored energy drink that Willow sold at her shop in Uptown.

"Because Phoebe said… Oh God." His stomach churned, and he suddenly felt like he might vomit.

"Dax, what is it?" Willow asked. "You look like you're going to be sick."

He *was* going to be sick. That meant that Phoebe's story didn't add up. She's said the Mastersons killed her brother, even showed her pictures of his death and told her they were going to kill her. Self-defense. Reasonable cause. But if she was lying… "I'm… fine."

Willow and Talisen continued to stare at him, waiting.

Dax cleared his throat. "I saw Phoebe today. I think she killed Maci Masterson."

Willow blinked at him. "Okay. I'm sure she had her reasons."

"She must have," Talisen agreed with a nod.

Dax's jaw tightened as he tapped his fingers on the wooden table in agitation. "That's what I thought too. But now… her actions don't add up. And I can't find any evidence that Maci Masterson did anything at all other than exist. No struggle, no crime, nothing but the death of one ordinary shifter." He picked up one of the cookies but didn't take a bite. "Phoebe said the Masterson pack killed her brother and were going to kill her too."

Willow and Talisen were silent as they let Dax's words sink in. Finally, Willow cleared her throat. "Seth is alive. I saw him today. Why does she think he's dead?"

"She said they showed her pictures," Dax said, knowing there could still be a reasonable explanation for why Phoebe killed the girl. He was just having trouble formulating it.

"That could've been forged," Willow insisted.

"You're right. It could've been." Dax rubbed his forehead, trying to ease the tension above his eyes. "Nothing adds up. She didn't tell either of us what was going on. Instead of using Void resources, she went to a safe house. The only reason I found her is because I had someone in tech track her credit card and was able to get a lead. She's must've ran out of cash, because today is the first time she used it. And then when I showed up at her safe house, she ran. Why would she run from me?"

Talisen and Willow shared a worried glance before Willow turned back to Dax. "I don't know. You're right—it is suspicious. But if she thinks her brother is dead, maybe she's having some sort of episode?"

"Maybe," Dax said, his heart sinking. "But whether that's true or not, I still have to bring her in, don't I?"

"He's right, Wil," Talisen said softly. "If Phoebe isn't thinking clearly, she's dangerous and needs help."

Willow stood up abruptly. "I just don't believe it. Phoebe would never kill someone unless it was self-defense."

"That's what I thought too," Dax said, feeling defeated. "But then today… I'm telling you, Wil, she wasn't herself."

Willow sat back in her chair, looking just as upset as Dax felt.

"Has she been here at all?" he asked her.

"Not that I know of, but I guess she could've come while I was at work." She glanced at Talisen. "Have you seen any signs of her?"

He shook his head. "I would've said something. But I also haven't exactly been looking for signs. Has anyone checked her room?"

Willow and Dax both shook their heads.

"Well, that's easy enough to do." Talisen got up and left the kitchen with Link following behind him.

Willow let out a long breath. "I just can't wrap my head around this. Are you really saying that you think she killed someone in cold blood?"

"No. I'm saying none of it adds up and now I'm in the fucked-up position of investigating my girlfriend."

Willow chewed on her bottom lip, closed her eyes, and shook her head. "I can't believe that. I won't. That's not Phoebe."

Dax stood. "You know, Willow, I agree with you. But what else am I going to do?"

A pained expression flashed over her face and she shook her head. "I don't know."

He grabbed the Mocha in Motion, downed the liquid, and said, "Thanks. Let me know if you hear anything."

"You too."

Dax left her at the table and went downstairs to join Talisen.

The fae was sitting at Phoebe's desk, an empty safe box in front of him. He glanced up, his green eyes full of worry. "This is her cash box."

Dax glanced at the empty metal box. "It's empty."

"All except this." He held up a bundle of papers. The top sheet had the corner ripped off.

"What is it?" He took it from Talisen and scanned the paperwork. It was a trust that listed her assets—including all her safe houses. The paper that had the torn corner was the safe house she'd been staying in the past few days. He frowned, still not able to make sense of anything. "So she took her emergency cash and couldn't remember the address of one of her safe houses, so she wrote it down?"

"That's what it looks like," Tal said. "Only Phoebe never forgets anything, especially something like this. Are you sure the woman you were with today was our Phoebe?"

God how he wished he'd been mistaken. "She sure the hell looked and sounded like her, Talisen."

"Spelled maybe?"

"I did have that thought. Either way, does it matter? I need to get her into the Void before she's hurt or she hurts someone else."

"Yeah." Talisen stood. "Let me know if you need any help, man. We love her too."

"I will." Dax shook the man's hand and took off, unable to spend another moment in Phoebe's space. It hurt too much.

Just as he was climbing into his Trooper, his phone buzzed. Leo's name flashed on the screen. He'd left Leo back at the Void that day to do more research on the Masterson pack. "Yeah?"

"We have a problem," the younger shifter said.

Dax turned the engine over and put the vehicle in gear. "What did you find?"

"Nothing. But we just got word there's been another attack. His name is Lincoln Frost, and he barely avoided a witch attack."

"Fuck. A death spell?"

"He doesn't know for sure, but he's in the infirmary due to a poison made with wolfsbane."

Wolfsbane. That's was one of the ingredients Phoebe had purchase that morning at the herb shop. "Are you there now?"

"Yes. Want me to meet you somewhere?" Leo asked.

"No. I'm on my way."

Chapter Fifteen

*A*llcot stood in the doorway of my studio, his gray eyes practically stalking me. I hid the betony wood behind my back, not wanting him to see I was experimenting with different herbs.

"Eadric. What can I do for you?" I asked, dropping the sprig on the worktable.

"I want you to come to bed," he said, keeping his eyes locked on mine.

"Do you think I've just forgotten how you manhandled me the other day?" I asked, my voice suddenly cold.

"No." He walked into the room and closed the door behind him. "I'm here to apologize."

"Some apology. I don't think I ever heard an 'I'm sorry.' The only thing I heard was that you wanted to get laid, so now you're doing whatever it takes."

He let out a low chuckle. "I love that fire, Phoebe. It's the reason I agreed to Seth's arrangement for us all those years ago."

I clamped my lips together, acutely aware that our

sparring was foreplay for him. Why hadn't I realized it before?

He stopped right in front of me and cupped my neck with his big hand, trailing his fingers over my pulse. It sped up and I silently cursed my body. I hated that his touch had that effect on me. There was no scenario in which I wanted Eadric Allcot, except when my body was betraying both my heart and my head.

I took a step back and sucked in a breath. "I'm not interested."

"Yes you are," he said, but he didn't make a move to invade my personal space again, thank the gods. "But I can see that you're still angry with me. How can I make it up to you?"

"Are you being serious right now?" I asked tentatively.

"Yes. I wouldn't offer if I didn't mean it." His gray eyes were intense, studying me.

I wanted to tell him to free Dax from the curse that bound him to the Red Door. But I knew that was a bad idea. Who knew what he'd do to Dax if he thought I cared too much? Instead, I said, "Let me work at the Red Door."

His eyes widened in surprise, and then he gave me the strangest look. "Now you're the one who can't be serious. No wife of mine is going to be sell herself to anyone, ever. Got that? If you want to pleasure someone, I'm the one you'll be getting on your knees for."

"Holy fuck, Allcot!" I straightened my entire body, lifting my chin in righteous indignation. "You think I want to sell my body for money? Have you lost your ever-loving mind?"

He frowned. "What else are you going to do there?"

I was still reeling from his assumption that I'd prostitute myself out. But then, why wouldn't he think that? The other

Phoebe had worked there for four years, albeit against her will. From Allcot's perspective, it was the last place I should be asking to work. I bit back a wince, realizing my mistake. I wanted to be there so I could help Dax. But I needed to come up with something else fast, or Allcot was going to get suspicious of my motives. "I just want to keep an eye on the girls. Make sure they're safe and treated right."

"I have bouncers for that," he said, crossing his arms over this chest.

I rolled my eyes. "Bouncers? You mean your vampires who don't have any idea what it's like for those women to leave themselves vulnerable to paying customers? They might be fine for when shit really goes down, but they won't be helpful when one of the girls gets a creepy vibe from someone or needs emotional support or advice on how to handle a tricky client. They won't understand what a woman needs to survive this industry." My tone had become soft, almost pleading. "I do. I can be the person watching out for them."

"You want to be the dorm mother," he said, finally understanding what I was getting at.

"Yeah, something like that."

He considered my proposal for what seemed like forever, both of us just staring at each other. Finally he asked, "Does this have anything to do with Marrok?"

"No." The lie rolled off my tongue effortlessly. He was the entire reason I wanted to be there. Though if I was planning on staying in this reality, I would be more than happy to use my Void skills to keep the customers in line. It seemed like a much worthier cause than hanging around the plantation, weeding the flower gardens.

"Fine," he barked out. When he spoke again, his voice

was full of venom. "But if I hear one word about you and Marrok, I'll kill him. You understand?"

A chill crawled up my spine. He meant it. There was no doubt about that. I had single-mindedly put Dax in very serious danger. Still I nodded, because if I didn't, it was likely Allcot would just kill Dax anyway. I was going to have to be very careful and make sure no one saw us talking beyond the polite niceties of a business owner to an employee. It would be tough, but I was well skilled at undercover operations. I'd just have to look at this in the same light.

"Good. Now that we have that settled, come here." He pointed to the space right in front of him. "It's time I collect my payment."

"Payment?" I scoffed. "And what's that exactly? If you're thinking you're getting a blow job, think again. I'm still not comfortable having your hands on me."

"There's no need for me to touch you if you're giving me a blow job," he said, his eyes on fire with lust now.

Shit. Stop it, Phoebs. The more I sassed him, the more turned on he seemed to get. "No thanks," I said flippantly. "I'm not in the mood."

He reached out, grabbed my wrist, and yanked me toward him. I had little choice but to let him. One hand circled my waist while the other caressed my jaw.

I felt nothing, thank the gods.

Or at least I didn't until he lowered his head and scraped his teeth over my pulse. My entire body flushed with heat, and my eyes closed at the erotic sensation.

"You like this," he breathed into my neck.

There was no point in denying it. I was certain the vampire could smell my reaction like a dog scenting steak on the barbeque. But that didn't mean I wanted to like it. I jerked away from him and clamped my hand over my tingling neck. "This… isn't going to happen."

"Maybe not today," he said with a cocky smile that made my stomach churn with unease. "But soon, my love. You'll forgive me and you'll be back in my bed, begging me to bite you."

I visibly shuddered. The memory of his fangs in my neck both excited and horrified me. I was a vampire hunter, for fuck's sake. Letting one bite me was *not* going to happen. Not again.

He let out a low chuckle, moved in closer again, and before I could make my escape, he dropped a light kiss on my temple, whispering, "You'll come for me soon, love. I know you and I know what you need."

Then he turned and was gone.

My blood ran cold. Was this what my life would be if I never got back to my reality? Years of fending off Allcot, or worse, giving in to him when he used his mesmerizing vamp powers on me? My skin crawled with the realization that my suspicions were probably correct. Life here would get really sticky, really fast. There wasn't any time to waste. I just prayed that Seth made it back sooner rather than later. He'd slipped into our world early in the morning, promising he'd track the other Phoebe, and one way or another, he'd bring her back. The fierce determination on his face had done little to comfort me. We both knew that my counterpart was just as powerful as I was, and if she didn't want to leave, Seth was going to have a bitch of a time forcing her. The only saving grace was that Seth was powerful too. I just hoped they didn't kill each other in the process.

THE RED DOOR was quiet in the early morning hours. The sun was just making its appearance in the hazy summer sky, but the humidity was already thick and oppressive. It was going to be the kind of day that just drained the energy right out of every living body. But I didn't care. I was free of Allcot for the moment, and because everyone except Dax was still asleep, I had him all to myself.

"Need some help?" I asked as I walked into the kitchen.

Dax's muscles flexed as he hauled in a couple of boxes of booze. His head jerked up at the sound of my voice, and a pleased smile claimed his full lips. "Good morning, Phoebe. What brings you here this fine morning?" But even as the words slipped out of his mouth, his eyes narrowed as he peered past me. "Is Allcot here?"

"No." Thank the gods. I'd gotten a ride with Pandora, who had gotten up early to head to a farmers' market. She'd said something about being first in line for the organic blueberries, or was it strawberries? I wasn't sure.

"He let you out of the house?" Dax asked, surprised.

I'd been surprised too when he'd agreed. But I wasn't going to argue. "Yep. I'm going to work here now."

Dax's eyes darkened and his mouth tightened, his entire body going taut. "What did you just say?"

"Dax, calm down. It's not a big deal—"

"The fuck it isn't! The entire reason you're with that asshole was so that you could get out of here. Now he's whoring you out? That's unacceptable and a breach of the contract. Does Seth know? What does he have to say about this? Or is he so far up Allcot's ass that he doesn't care?"

His rant was so impressive, I hadn't even thought to stop him. But now he was glaring at me as if I'd done something wrong. "Chill out, big guy," I said, placing my hand gently on his chest. "No one is forcing me to do anything. I'm here to make sure the girls are taken care of. You know, make sure no one gets out of line and that they have someone to talk to when a sensitive matter comes up."

Dax's eyebrows pinched together as he stared at me in confusion. "Allcot asked you to keep an eye on the girls?"

I shook my head and smiled gently. "No. I asked him to let me."

"Oh." His shoulders relaxed, and he regarded me with something that looked a lot like appreciation, or maybe it was admiration. It was hard to tell. "I see. That makes some sense. You know what it's like to work here. You can relate."

I couldn't. Not really. But that was a story for a different day. "I just want to be helpful. To them and..." I glanced around, checking to be sure we really were alone. Then I lowered my voice and said, "And to you. Listen, Dax, if there was a chance someone could break that spell that binds you here, would you want them to do it? Even if it meant betraying Allcot and you had to leave New Orleans for your own safety?"

He let out a surprised bark of laughter. "Are you kidding? Fuck yes. You got someone in mind?"

I nodded slowly.

Suspicion crept into his gaze and he shook his head. "No, Phoebe. You can't. It's too dangerous. I won't let you put yourself in that position. Allcot will..." He cleared his throat. "You know what he will do."

I wanted so badly to say *What if I said I'd be leaving too?* But the truth was my doppelgänger would be back, and to everyone else, nothing would've ever changed. "We could make it look like someone else helped you."

He blinked down at me, hope and fear and something

else passing through his eyes. His voice was raw and full of emotion when he said, "You know he'll never believe that."

I shook my head. "You don't know that. If we can break the curse, we can figure out how to keep my involvement hidden."

"I won't let you. I'm not leaving here while you're still trapped with him," he insisted.

My heart nearly broke in two. This man, the one who mirrored the man I loved in every way that mattered, loved my doppelgänger so much he was willing to give up everything for her. But what had she tried to do for him? Did it matter to her at all that he was trapped here because he was trying to protect her? That wasn't something I was going to get answered, and likely the truth was far more complicated than I would care to admit. I sucked in a fortifying breath. "What I want to know is, if you knew I'd be safe and you had a chance to break free, would you take it? Don't analyze this or come up with scenarios why it won't work, just tell me your truth."

It took him a while to answer, but when he did, he said, "If I was positive you'd be safe, then yes. I'd break free from here and never look back."

Chapter Sixteen

"*W*here is he?" Dax said the moment he strode into the healer's office.

Leo quickly stood. "Imogen is with him in the back."

"Let's go." Dax took the lead, ignoring the protests of the receptionist.

"Sir, you can't go back there," she said, running to catch up with him. "The exam rooms are private."

"We're with the Arcane," he said and knocked once on the closed exam room door.

"Come in, Kelly," Imogen called from the other side of the door.

The receptionist brushed past them, giving Dax a glare and poking her head in. "Two men from the Arcane are here."

"Thanks, Kel. Send them in."

Kelly grimaced and whispered to Dax and Leo, "This is completely against protocol. Next time let me ask first."

"Sure thing," Leo said, smiling down at her. "It's just been one of those days, you know?"

Her expression softened. "I get it." Then she brushed her fingers over his arm before she glided back down the hallway.

Dax rolled his eyes. "You couldn't have pulled the charm out five minutes earlier?"

Leo shrugged one shoulder. "It helps to be good cop when you're around, biting people's heads off."

"Dax?" Imogen called. "Is everything all right? Is Phoebe okay?"

The man on the table flinched when Imogen said Phoebe's name.

Dax ignored the healer's question and walked over to the patient. "Hello. Are you Lincoln Frost?"

"Who wants to know?" the shifter growled.

"Sorry," Imogen said, sliding off her rolling stool. "Lincoln, this is Dax Marrok and Leo Shepard. They work for the Arcane, and I'm sure they're here to ask you about your attack."

"We are," Dax said, never taking his eyes from the man. He held his hand out. "Thank you for speaking with us today, Mr. Frost."

The shifter glanced at Dax's hand but made no move to take it. "I haven't agreed to do anything, Mr. Marrok."

Dax sighed and pulled up a chair. "Do you mind telling me why you're reluctant to file a report about your attack?"

"Oh, I don't know. Maybe because my attacker works for you?"

Dax felt a growl rumbling in the back of his throat, but he swallowed it. His reaction was due to Phoebe's actions, not the shifter's reluctance. Hell, Dax would be wary too if he was in the other man's shoes.

"I'm here to get to the truth, Mr. Frost. I assure you, we're taking this very seriously. If Agent Kilsen is behind an illegal attack, she will be brought in."

"Phoebe did this?" Imogen whispered. "Oh my god."

Leo made some sort of confirming noises.

Dax peered at the guy. His coloring was gray and he had the gaunt look of a man who wasn't long for this life. He just prayed that Imogen was able to reverse the wolfsbane poisoning. "Can you tell me what happened?"

"Sure. Your girl attacked me. I was leaving work and had just stepped off the elevator into the parking garage. She came out of nowhere, punched me in the kidney, and then stabbed me with a fucking needle. Ten minutes later, the world was spinning and I was puking my guts out. Now I get to take these fucking herbs for the next year and hope the wolfsbane didn't fuck up my heart. Then there's the silver particles. They'll keep me weak for the next several weeks, so life is just going to be peachy after I tell my boss I'm going to miss work for the next month."

Dax glanced at Imogen for confirmation.

The healer nodded.

Fucking hell. Attempted murder. "I hope you have a full recovery, Mr. Frost. Wolfsbane and silver—that's a powerful combination."

"No shit," the man muttered.

Dax pulled out his notebook. "If you don't mind, I'd like to ask a few more questions."

"There's really nothing else to say, but go ahead."

"Have you ever met Agent Kilsen or seen her before today?" Dax asked.

"Not in person." He shook his head. "I've seen her in the papers though. She lives with that fairy who runs a nonprofit, right?"

"Right." Willow had a charity that's sole mission was to raise money for the new supernatural hospital project in New Orleans.

"Yeah, anyway. Us wolves like to keep tabs on the witches in the city. We all know who she is."

Dax narrowed his eyes at the man. He himself was a shifter, and while it was true he knew who all the witches were, he only knew because it was part of his job. "Why, exactly?"

"One has to know in case they get jumped on the street," Frost said dryly.

"Does that happen often?" Dax's tone was matter-of-fact, but inside he was seething. He hated the way the man was sneering about witches. At the same time, he hated that Phoebe had proven him right. But most of all he hated that he had no idea why Phoebe had attacked the man.

"What? Witches attacking shifters?"

"Yes, that."

"No. At least not that I know of. But it used to. We always figured it was just a matter of time before we became targets again." Frost leaned back against the wall and pressed his hand to his chest. "Damn. I need to sleep for a week."

"Oh no you don't," Imogen said, rushing to his side and pushing a needle into his arm.

Frost let out a sigh of relief and gave Imogen a pleased smile. "You sure know how to treat a man."

She patted him on the arm. "You just keep resting."

Dax wondered again why Phoebe had targeted the shifters. His comment about witches fit with the pack's previous prejudices. It wasn't crazy to think they still harbored those feelings. But as far as Dax knew, they hadn't acted on them or given Phoebe any reason to attack.

"One last question," Dax said.

"Just this one," Imogen said, frowning. "He really does need his rest."

"Sure." He turned his gaze on the ashen man. "To the best of your knowledge, has anyone else in your pack had contact or any altercations with Agent Kilsen?"

"I can't speak for everyone." He yawned and his eyes started to water. "But not that I know of."

Dax flipped his notebook closed, held his hand out to the man, and said, "Thank you for your time. I appreciate your cooperation."

This time Frost reached out and shook Dax's hand. His grip was surprisingly strong for a man who'd just been poisoned. "A word of advice?"

Dax raised his eyebrows and waited.

"Bring in your girlfriend sooner rather than later, otherwise the pack will take matters into their own hands." He jerked his hand away and let out a snarl.

Dax stared him down, unwilling to take the bait. Of course they knew he and Phoebe had a relationship. They were keeping tabs on the witches of the town, and Phoebe and Dax weren't taking any pains to keep the information hidden. It did explain why Dax didn't socialize with them though. If they were still harboring their witch hate, they weren't the type of shifters he was interested in knowing. He did find it curious the shifter made a point of issuing a threat.

"Thanks for the warning." Dax glanced at Leo and jerked his head toward the door. "Imogen, if I can have a word?"

"I'll be right out," she said.

Dax and Leo left the room.

Leo's face was full of apprehension and he opened his mouth to say something, but Dax put his hand up, stopping him. They definitely shouldn't be talking about the case at Imogen's.

"We'll talk about it later," Dax said.

"Right."

The door opened and Imogen walked out, carrying a chart. Her lips were pursed and she looked like she'd just eaten something sour.

"Are you all right?" Dax asked.

"Fine," she said sarcastically. "You do your best to keep a shifter from dying on your exam table and he repays you by grabbing your ass. But sure. I'm good."

Leo pushed off the wall and made a move to head back into the room, but Imogen stepped in his path, cutting him off.

"I handled it. I might have also mentioned that Allcot is an investor in the clinic and that he doesn't take kindly to shifters harassing the healers."

Leo snorted.

Dax's lips twitched. He liked a woman who wasn't afraid to put a jackass in his place. "I bet he loved that."

"Let's just say he's not super pleased a clinic supported by a vampire might have saved his life. That one appears to have some very strange ideas about the hierarchy of supernaturals."

"He's a bigot," Dax said. "Even so, that doesn't warrant a poisoning attack."

"Do you really think Phoebe did it?" Imogen asked in a hushed whisper.

Unfortunately, he did. He nodded. "What I need to know is how she was before she left your office last week. Was she on any medication that might cause her to... act in an unusual manner?"

"No. She wasn't on anything. In fact, I'd given her a clean bill of health." Imogen frowned. "You think her actions are drug related?"

Leo sucked in a sharp breath. "Not Phoebe. Surely she wouldn't—"

"It's a possibility, Leo," Dax said, his tone grave. "In some ways, I hope it is. At least then we'd have an explanation."

"I'll check her chart, just to be sure." Imogen hurried down the hall, gesturing for them to follow her into a room with files lining the walls. It took her a few moments of digging, but then she said, "Aha! There it is. She might've been taking… Oh, no. Just a little herb concoction to aid in healing."

It was Dax's turn to suck in a long breath. "All right. Thanks, Imogen."

She gave him a sympathetic smile. "I hope you find her and that this is all a giant misunderstanding."

"Sure. Me too." It was going to have to be the biggest fucking misunderstanding ever if he didn't want to be the one to put his girlfriend in jail.

Chapter Seventeen

*A*fter my talk with Dax that morning, I wasn't sure where that left me with my plan to free him from Allcot's service. If I found a way to free him, then when Seth brought the other Phoebe back, she'd still be with Allcot. But Dax would be gone. Would Allcot blame her? Would she be in danger?

Neither Dax nor I wanted that scenario. He wouldn't be able to live with himself if his actions put her in danger. I didn't feel quite as strongly about it. She had taken my place in my world after all. But I did see why she'd want to run from her oppressive life. Straight up forgiveness wasn't in the cards, but understanding might be.

I spent the rest of the quiet morning avoiding Dax. Talking was painful for both of us. But it would be worse if Allcot found out. That bastard. I hated thinking of what he might do to Dax if I fucked up.

Still, I couldn't just do nothing. It wasn't in my nature. After making the rounds to the girls' rooms to let them know

I was there for whatever they needed, I slipped into Willow's room and sat on the edge of her bed.

"Hey," she said, giving me a small smile. "What are you doing here?"

"Keeping an eye on you." I squeezed her hand, trying not to think about what her life had become here. "Are you okay?"

"Sure. I was just flipping through this course catalog. I think I'm going to sign up for a culinary class."

My heart warmed. "That will be absolutely perfect for you."

"Isn't it?" She sighed and opened the catalog to a page near the front. "It's at the New Orleans Institute of Cuisine. They offer a full course load and at the end, if I pass, I'll get a chance to work at some of the finest restaurants in the city. I'd have to work my way up of course, but I could be working with herbs." Her eyes glittered with excitement. "Can you imagine? Me a head chef at Chez Willow?"

I laughed. "Sure. Or running your own bakery."

She pressed a hand to her heart and sighed. "Wouldn't that just be lovely?"

"It'd be perfect," I said with a nod, hoping that little seed sprouted and grew in the future.

Willow's eyes filled with tears as she looked at me. "None of this would've been possible without you. Thank you."

I wasn't sure how to respond to that. Sure, Allcot had given the girls new contracts because I'd balked at their treatment, but if I had my way, if any of them wanted to leave for a better life, I'd have given them money to do it. But Allcot wasn't so generous with his cash. I supposed that's what made him a successful businessman, but it didn't mean I had to like that he owned a gentleman's club.

"I didn't do anything special," I said quietly. "In fact, I wanted to do a whole lot more."

Willow squeezed my hand. "You did what you could. That's what's important."

"Right." I slid off the bed and glanced around the room. "Do you think I could ask you a favor?"

"Sure, honey. Anything."

"Are you still in charge of making aphrodisiacs for the clients? Edible ones?"

Her cheeks turned pink and she plucked at the bedspread. "Yeah. Did you need something for Eadric?"

"Oh gods no!" I cried, feeling scandalized. "Ugh. Never."

Her lips twitched into a tiny smile as she looked up at me. "That didn't sound like a wife who's dying to hop into bed with her husband."

"You can say that again," I muttered.

Her amusement vanished and her expression turned concerned. "Is it really that bad?"

The memory of his teeth on my neck came roaring back and my skin started to tingle again. I didn't have the answer to her question, but I could guess. "No, I suppose not. I just... the marriage isn't something I chose, you know?"

"I do. I just thought... you two have been together for four years. I hate to think of you in a sexless marriage. That's not you. It never was."

I couldn't imagine being in a sexless relationship either. And all evidence pointed to the fact that my doppelgänger did in fact share Allcot's bed. But I wouldn't. There was no way I was going to let him coax me into his bed. That was a hard pass. "No. It isn't," I agreed. "But anyway, that's not why I was asking."

"Oh?" One eyebrow rose in curiosity. "Then why?"

"I'm working on a couple of potions, and my supply at home is lacking some key ingredients. I was hoping I could check out your stash. See if anything jumps out at me."

"Sure." She hopped off the bed, shoved her feet into a pair of fuzzy slippers, and led me out of her room, down the stairs, and to a locked door next to a storage closet. She pressed her palm to the wood just above the knob and said, "Willow Rhoswen."

The door swung open, seemingly of its own free will, and without missing a beat, I hightailed it into Willow's workspace. Massive amounts of herbs and specialty concoctions filled the shelves. "Oh wow," I said, my eyes wide with surprise. "Did Allcot let you buy all this stuff?"

She shook her head and laughed. "No way. Clio did. She was having me make all kinds of potions and herb bundles and... Well, never mind. Let's just say she decided I was the most talented magic user of her girls and had me making all kinds of questionable potions and spells."

"Ones she used on the staff," I guessed.

"Yeah." The one word hung in the air between us. It meant Willow's magic was at the heart of all of Clio's curses.

Nausea rolled through my stomach. "Did she force *you* to spell people?"

A single tear rolled down her cheek as she nodded again.

"Oh, honey. It's not your fault," I said earnestly.

"It's my magic that bound them here," she said, barely able to get the words out.

"Oh my god, Willow," I said, my voice rising in excitement. "You know what this means?"

She turned to me, startled. "No. What?"

"You can break the binding that holds Dax to this place. All you have to do is reverse the spell."

Her rosy cheeks turned pasty white, and she shook her head as she started to back up. "I can't do that," she said in the barest of whispers. "You know I can't. Eadric would…" She shook her head harder. "I'd be punished. What about my classes?"

Son of a… I bit back a curse and tried to hold it together. The Willow in my world wouldn't have hesitated. She'd already be working on a way to undo any damage she'd caused. It was strange to see this one so frightened. Though I supposed if you were repressed enough, fear had a way of digging in and sinking its hooks into you.

"It's okay, Wil," I said gently. "I'm not asking you to do anything that would get you into trouble. I don't want that for you. Neither would Dax. Let's just think this through, okay?"

"Yeah, okay, sure," she said, taking a deep breath. "Think it through." She turned her bright blue eyes on me. "Think what through, exactly?"

"Let's just think through how to explain why the binding would fail. That's all. A brainstorming session if you will."

"Brainstorming. Right. Okay." She bit down on her bottom lip. "Does he want to leave?"

I gave her a what-the-fuck look. "Yeah, Wil. He doesn't want to be under Allcot's thumb for the rest of his life, just like you don't."

"But isn't his contract for a year, just like the rest of us?"

"No." I tilted my head studying her. "Is that what you thought?"

"Sure. Everyone else got the same deal. Why not him? I figured he'd work his year and then take the bonus like the rest of us."

Allcot hadn't offered him any such deal. Dax would've told me when we talked earlier. And I was pretty certain I knew why. It all came down to my counterpart. The other Phoebe. Allcot and Dax both wanted her, and Allcot would not lose. I stared at Willow, my expression hard and my voice cold. "Allcot is punishing him because he cares about me. I won't stand for it. I can't, Wil. You understand that, right?"

"Sure. Absolutely," she said, nodding.

"Okay, good. Then you don't mind if I experiment with some of your herbs?"

Willow swept her gaze over her worktable, looking from me to her stash. She pressed her hand to her forehead and said, "Yeah. I mind. But only because it will only take me about half an hour to make the potion. And likely if you do it, it won't even work. Breaking a fae spell is trickier than breaking one made by a witch."

All the tension drained from my shoulders, and I grabbed her, pulling her in for a fierce hug. "Thank you, Wil."

"You're welcome. But while I'm doing this, you better come up with a damned good excuse as to why the binding failed. Otherwise, we're all going to be in a heap of shit."

"I'm on it."

Twenty minutes later, she handed me a pale pink potion and I handed her the bottle of dragon's blood.

"What's this?" she asked me.

"Take a look at the expiration date on the bottom."

She turned it over and frowned. "This says it expired six months ago."

"Right. If Allcot asks what happened, you feign innocence and tell him you need to check on something. Tear through your studio and finally come up with this. It's the active ingredient in binding spells, right?"

"Sure. But it lasts forever," she said, still staring at the bottom of the bottle.

I shrugged. "Clio bought you discount products. It's not your fault. You just used what you were given."

A slow smile broke out on her face as my words sank in. Then she threw her head back and laughed. "You're brilliant, Phoebe. Clio was cheap as shit. Everyone who knew her knew that. And since Allcot hasn't allowed me to source my own herbs, it's not my fault either. This is perfect."

I threw my arms around her one more time, squeezing her tight, and said, "I love you, Wil. You're the best kind of person."

"I love you too, Phoebe," she said with a sniffle. "Now go. Let Dax know he has his freedom when he's ready."

Chapter Eighteen

"You're sure you want to do this?" Director Halston said as she read Dax's report.

"Am I sure?" Dax scoffed and started to pace the director's office. "No. I'm not even remotely sure I want to turn that in. But it's increasingly clear that the people on that list are in danger, and all roads lead back to Kilsen."

The director rubbed her chin. "Kilsen has never given me any indication that she's anything other than a dedicated agent. Are we sure this isn't a setup?"

"I thought of that. More than a few times. None of this is like Kilsen. And if I hadn't seen her yesterday, I'd still assume she was undercover for a reason. But she was cagey, acting very strange, and then she ghosted. That isn't…" He wanted to scream. The fact that even the director was questioning his conclusions was enough to send him right over the fucking edge. "She's never lied about or kept anything from me about an investigation before. It doesn't make sense that she wouldn't turn to me, or even you and the Void if she was innocent."

"Perhaps." The director had a thoughtful look on her face. "But, in any case, you're right. She has to be brought in. We can't leave a rogue agent out in the wind carrying out some secret mercenary mission. Do what you have to do to bring her in."

"Yes, ma'am," he said and stopped wearing a hole in the carpet. "I also want to bring the shifters on the list in for protection until we find her."

"You're that concerned?"

"One is dead and another was poisoned today. I think we have a moral obligation to protect them."

Halston dropped the file on her desk. "You're right. We do. I'll have Maria issue an order. Give her a few hours. This requires clearance from the higher-ups."

"Thank you." Dax walked out of the office, feeling defeated even though the director had given him everything he'd asked for. The problem was, he both did and didn't want to be responsible for bringing in Phoebe. He loved her. Wanted her safe. But if she was behind the attacks, he had no choice. And he'd prefer it be him that brought her in rather than any of the other agents. He'd handle her with care. The others, they'd use the opportunity to air any grievances. And Phoebe and her give-no-fucks attitude had certainly earned some enemies.

No, if he handled it, he'd be able to make sure she wasn't hurt. He'd also be able to get a psych evaluation just to be on the safe side.

Instead of pacing the Void building, waiting for the orders to come through or for someone to call in with a tip on Phoebe's movements in the city, Dax slipped back into investigation mode. He needed to retrace the steps of the victim and figure out what happened before her death. Try to see why she and Phoebe ended up in an altercation. He only had the vague information that Phoebe had supplied. She'd insisted shifters had shown up with pictures of her dead brother and threatened her. If it was true, he needed to track who else had threatened her and why. He'd start at the scene of the crime and work backward.

"Leo?" Dax called as he walked back into his office.

"Yeah, boss?" The young shifter lifted his head from the files he was studying.

"We're headed into the field. Time for some old-school research." He jerked his head, indicating the shifter should follow.

"Where are we headed?" Leo asked, falling into step beside Dax.

"Back to the beginning."

DAX AND LEO stood on the sidewalk next to the cemetery. There wasn't anything to even hint there'd been a death in the area less than a week ago. Dax hadn't expected there to be.

"You studied the files," he said to Leo. "Didn't Maci work around here?"

"Yes. At an interior design firm on Magazine." He pulled out his phone and checked his notes. "Old World Elegance."

"Lead the way."

A green velvet couch with a scalloped, tufted back was the showpiece in the firm's reception area along with two matching armchairs. A clean-cut young man who'd been sitting behind an ornate wood banker's desk rose and walked over to the two shifters.

"Good afternoon," the dark-haired man with kind eyes said, holding his hand out. "I'm Drake. Do you have an appointment?"

Dax shook the man's hand. "Hello, Drake. I'm Dax, and this is my associate Leo. We don't have an appointment. We were just hoping to ask a few questions."

"Sure. Do you have a place that needs to be decorated? Or are you looking for a few key pieces?"

"Neither." Dax pulled a business card out of his pocket and handed it over. "We work for the Arcane, and we're investigating Maci Masterson's death. I understand she worked here."

The man's expression turned to one of despair and his eyes turned too bright. "Yeah," he croaked. "She worked here. In fact, that's the reason I'm working the front desk. That was her job."

"What do you normally do?" Dax asked, just to ease the man into the conversation. He was clearly shaken up, and Dax wondered if Drake and Maci might have had more than just a working relationship.

"Stockroom stuff. Inventory. Deliveries. That kind of thing."

Dax nodded. "Were you working the day of her death?"

"Yes, sir. Maci helped me check in a large order." He swallowed hard. "We spend most of the day together. She was headed out for drinks with a guy from school. She was really excited about it."

That didn't sound like a woman who was planning to threaten a witch. Dax frowned. "Did the guy come here to pick her up?"

He shook his head. "No, they were going to meet some place uptown that isn't far from the streetcar line. That's why she was headed up to Saint Charles. Usually I give her a ride home, but I stayed late to finish some work." The young man stared at his feet. "I should've just taken her like usual. The work could've waited."

"I'm sorry for your loss," Leo said, clapping the guy on the shoulder. "It's not your fault, you know."

Drake turned blazing eyes on Leo. "What would you know about it? My... friend is dead and I could've prevented it. She was a sweet girl who only wanted to finish school and get a job at a prominent architecture firm. Fuck." He pressed his hands to his eyes, clearly trying to keep the tears at bay. "She was the last person who deserved this."

Dax was certain the kid had been in love with her. All the signs were there. He waited until Drake dropped his hands and took a deep breath.

"Sorry. I just can't believe she's gone," Drake said.

"I know it's hard," Dax said, clamping down on his own emotions. Phoebe wasn't physically gone from this world, but the one he knew and had fallen for appeared to be lost. "Can you tell me if she's ever had any trouble? Any enemies or tumultuous relationships? In other words, is there anyone we should be looking at closer as a suspect?"

"No," Drake said, frowning. "No one. Everyone loved her."

Including Drake. Since Dax already knew who'd killed her, he didn't expect this kid to come up with anyone new, but he continued the line of questioning. "What about her date? The guy she was supposed to have drinks with?"

He shook his head. "No way, man. He's my cousin, another shifter who just moved to town right before the semester started. They barely knew each other."

Another dead end. Dax had been pressing to uncover

acquaintances that might be involved in Seth's death, or a secret past. But there was just nothing there. "Thanks for your time. You've been very helpful. Is there anyone else here we can talk to? Just to be thorough?"

Drake nodded and disappeared into the back to fetch his boss.

By the time Dax and Leo left the office, Maci Masterson had been painted as a sweet angel with zero skeletons in her closet.

With his last shred of hope that maybe Phoebe wasn't the villain in this nightmare completely shredded, Dax ducked his head and was silent on his way back to the Trooper. Leo was too, and Dax knew the kid was thinking the same. Now the only thing left to do was rip his own heart out while he brought down the one woman he'd ever cared about.

His phone chimed, giving the go-ahead to pick up the other three shifters on the list. Since Lincoln Frost had already been attacked and he knew where that shifter was located, that meant he only needed to track down the other two. Without a word, Dax put the Trooper in gear and headed to the Lakeview neighborhood.

"I'M NOT GOING," Gerry Coster said. He was standing in the doorway of his Gothic-style two-story Tudor home. "I'm not afraid of a witch."

Leo raised his eyebrows. "That witch has already taken down two of your pack."

He shrugged, squinting back at them as the afternoon light illuminated his bald head. "I have a family to protect. If she's targeting me, what's to say she won't go after my daughter if I'm hiding at the Arcane building?"

Dax had to admit the guy had a point. It would take an act of God to get him to leave his own family vulnerable... if he had one. He peered past the round, middle-aged man. "Is your daughter here? We can probably request security to keep an eye on her and the rest of your family."

"No, she isn't. She lives with her mother in Mississippi."

Dammit, Dax thought. He'd just used his kid as an excuse. "I really think you should consider our offer, Mr. Coster. Agent Kilsen is deemed very dangerous. If you don't—"

"I'm not going with you. End of story." Coster slammed the door in their faces.

Their reception was very much the same at Prim Masterson's home a few miles away.

"I've fought witches before, Mr. Marrok," Prim said, standing with her shoulders back and her head held high. "I used to be in law enforcement." The woman appeared to be in her late thirties, early forties, and was dressed in linen pants and a silk camisole. Her auburn hair was twisted into a smart bun, and she looked like she'd be at home running a multimillion-dollar business.

"I understand, but she's already attacked two of your pack. Are you sure you want to take that risk? She's a highly trained agent," Dax said.

"I'm a highly trained judo master. While I appreciate your concern, I'll have to decline your protection."

She couldn't be budged. When the door was slammed in their faces for the second time that day, Dax muttered a curse.

"Idiots," Leo said under his breath.

Dax let out a snort of agreement. He understood their pride. Shifters were convinced they could take care of themselves, but they didn't know Phoebe like he did.

At least Frost had been willing. After his brush with the poison, he didn't even out up a fight when Dax visited him at Imogen's clinic.

"Good. We'll move you today," Dax said, relieved at least one of the targets would be safe. With the approval from the higher-ups, Phoebe Kilsen's clearance at the Void offices had been revoked. She wouldn't even be allowed in unless she was being incarcerated. Frost would be safe there.

Once Frost was settled, Dax turned to Leo. "Are you up for a stakeout?"

"Always," Leo said.

"Good. Because you're taking Coster. I'll take Prim Masterson. If Phoebe shows up, do not engage. Call for backup first," Dax ordered.

"What if she goes after Coster?" Leo asked.

"Pray backup gets there sooner," Dax said solemnly.

"But—"

"I'm serious, Leo. Phoebe is a powerful witch who's beyond reason right now. Coster refused protection. I will not have you risking your life because he's a stubborn bastard."

"Okay, boss," Leo said. "But I need a car."

Dax secured one of the Void vehicles for Leo, and the two split up to spend the night keeping an eye on Prim Masterson and Gerry Coster.

But just as Dax pulled up to Prim's house, he got the call. Gerry Coster was dead.

Chapter Nineteen

"Hey, Phoebe. There you are," a tinkling feminine voice called as I was walking down the hallway from Willow's work station.

I turned and found Genevieve smiling at me. "Hey, Gen. What can I do for you?"

"I need a favor," the club manager said. "Can you stick around for a while?"

The clock on the far wall indicated it was just after six in the evening. I'd already been there for roughly twelve hours. Not that I minded. It was better than being back at the plantation, playing the Southern belle to Eadric Allcot. "Sure. I'm not in a hurry. What do you need?"

She let out a visible sigh of relief, her shoulders sagging. "Oh, thank the gods. I have an errand to run for Allcot and no one to cover the bar for the next couple of hours. Can you take it for me like you used to?"

"Sure. No problem. I'm really rusty, but it'll all probably come rushing back once I get into the groove."

"Thank you," she gushed. "You're a lifesaver. I'll be back as soon as I can."

I watched the petite redhead hurry out of the club and wondered what it was Allcot needed from her. But then I caught a glimpse of Dax disappearing up the stairs and I hurried after him. I caught up to him just before he stepped into the large office that had become Allcot's.

"Hey, Dax," I said.

He paused, his hand on the doorknob. When he turned, his dark eyes were soft and welcoming. "Hi."

The rough sound of his voice combined with that all-too-familiar look he was giving me made me suddenly ache for my Dax back home. My mouth went dry as I gazed up at him, and I had to lick my lips just to get them moving again.

His gaze moved to my mouth, and his soft eyes turned heated. Before either of us said anything, he glanced away. "I'm supposed to be stocking the fridge in there." He pointed to Allcot's office. "Is there something you need?"

"Huh?" I asked like the idiot I was.

"You wanted something?" he asked again, his eyebrows raised.

"Oh, right." I let out a startled laugh. What the hell was wrong with me? "Let's talk inside the office."

"Sure." He used one of the master keys to open the door. After flipping the light on, he waved me in. "What's up?"

I slipped my hand into the front pocket of my jeans and produced the small container of the potion Willow had made earlier in the day. "This is for you." I pressed it into the palm of his hand and leaned in close, whispering, "It will break the spell that binds you to the Red Door. Willow made it for you, so it's pretty much guaranteed to work."

He jerked back and stared down at me, his eyes wide in shock. *Willow made it?* he mouthed.

Clearly we were both on the same page. Neither of us wanted any curious eavesdroppers listening in on our conversation. I nodded and whispered, "We've got it worked out. She won't be blamed. Take it when you're ready."

His hand circled around my wrist as he closed his eyes and said, "What about you?"

"I'll be fine," I insisted. "Trust me."

He opened his eyes and stared down at me, emotion swimming in his dark depths. "I can't leave knowing you're still tied to him."

"You can. And you will, Dax," I said earnestly. "You gave up eight years of your life already. There isn't anything else you can do. Please, take this and find happiness, live, be kind to yourself. Ph—" I cleared my throat, having almost referred to my doppelgänger. "*I* have Seth. He'll watch over me."

"You're sure. Are you really safe, Phoebe?"

"I'm as safe as I can be, Dax." I pressed a soft hand to his chest and gazed up at him. "All I want is for you to be happy and free from Allcot."

His lips curved down as he frowned.

"What is it?" I asked.

"I'm not sure how I'm going to get out of this town. It's not like I've been paid these last years."

"Dammit. Really?"

He nodded solemnly. "I can probably hitch a ride up to Baton Rouge and catch some work there, but—"

"No." I cut him off and shook my head. "I'll find some money for you. Or something to sell. Don't worry about that. Just give me until tomorrow. Okay?"

"I can't let you—"

"You're not letting me doing anything. I'm just doing it. Now drink up, got it?" I nudged his hand.

"Yes, ma'am," he said, his lips twitching again. "I always did like it when you were bossy."

Welcome to the club, I thought. "I know. And you always knew how to shut me up too."

Silence hung heavily in the air between us, each of us lost in thought. It had been a stupid thing to say. This Dax wasn't my Dax, and I had no business strolling down memory lane with him.

I stepped back. "Sorry."

"It's all right."

I shook my head and removed my hand from his chest. "No, it isn't."

"It is," he said with a small smile. Then he lifted the potion to his lips and downed it. The effect was immediate. A single pinpoint of light appeared and then zoomed around his wrists and ankles as if shackling him, then moved to encircle his entire body, coiling around him like a rope.

I took a step back, my hand covering my open mouth. "What did Willow do?" I whispered, having no idea how to stop the alarming light that seemed to be tightening around his core.

Dax's eyes went wide, and he let out a grunt as he winced.

"Oh my god, Dax. I'm so sorry. This isn't what's supposed to happen." I started to run for the door, intending to grab Willow wherever she was.

My hand had just hit the doorknob when Dax grunted, "Wait."

"But I—" I turned just in time to see the rope of light constrict, squeezing him so tightly that his face turned red. "What, Dax?"

He lifted his head and wheezed, "Just. Wait."

I did as he asked, hating every minute of it. The light pulsed, seemingly only to torture him, tightening each time just a little more. "Dax, please. I need to get Wil—"

There was a small boom, and the light dissipated all around the room.

Dax let out a whoosh of air only to quickly gasp for more, trying to fill his exhausted, battered lungs.

"Oh my god," I said in a hushed tone, gingerly moving toward him. "Are you okay?"

He sucked in one more deep breath and straightened, holding his arms out, inspecting them.

"Dax?"

A huge grin broke out over his face, and he reached for me, scooping me up into a giant bear hug and twirling me around the room while letting out a giant whoop of excitement.

"Dax," I said again, laughing. "Shhh. Someone is going to hear you."

He stopped twirling and just stared down at me. "It worked, Phoebs. It really worked. When the rope of light burst apart, my invisible chains disappeared too. I'm free. Finally, after all these years, I'm free."

Happiness bubbled up in the form of delighted laughter, and I hugged him so tight I thought we might just meld there together as one.

But it didn't take long for me to become aware of his breathing, his woodsy scent, and the fact that he felt so damned good as I rested my head against his shoulder, still suspended in the air by his strong arms.

"Phoebe?" he whispered.

I lifted my head and looked up at him. "Yeah?"

"Thank you."

His husky, gruff voice was like a caress to my weary soul, and I couldn't help myself as I reached up and pressed my fingertips to his lips. He kissed them tenderly, just as I knew he would, and then I dropped my hand, intending to ask to be put down, but Dax leaned in closer and suddenly his lips were on mine. I melted right into him, getting lost in his warm vanilla taste. Without my even realizing it, he slowly lowered me back down until my feet hit the floor, and then one hand was in my hair while the other was caressing my back.

The kiss was hot, full of fire and need and desperation. The way two people come together when they've been longing for each other for far too long. My hands were in his thick dark hair, caressing his shoulders, his back, and were headed south when the sound of a door opening made us both freeze.

I held my breath and waited, praying it was Willow or even Genevieve. But no. My blood ran cold when I heard Allcot's low, rumbling voice behind me say, "Step away from my wife."

Chapter Twenty

"Wait!" Prim Masterson ran out of her house, her arm in the air. The linen pants and silk camisole had been replaced by jeans and a T-shirt. The blood had drained from her face, and fear shone in her light eyes. She yanked his passenger door open and climbed in. "I'm coming with you."

Dax didn't say a word as he took off toward Castor's house. The minute he'd gotten word about the other shifter's death, he'd walked to her door, given her the news, and then offered to take her in again. She'd immediately refused. It had pissed him off, but he'd just nodded and jogged back to the Trooper.

It hadn't taken long for her to change her mind, which was good, because he wasn't slowing down for anyone. The Trooper came to a screeching stop in front of the Gothic Tudor home. Void agents were milling around everywhere while Leo sat on the front steps, his head in his hands.

"Hey," Dax said to him. "What happened?"

Leo jerked his head up and grimaced. "She was here, Dax."

"I gathered that since Coster is dead," Dax said, his stomach churning. "Did you see her?"

"I saw her fleeing. She was wearing a blond wig and was dressed in scrubs like she'd just gotten off a shift at a hospital, but I know for sure it was her. She looked right at me. There was no mistaking those bright blue eyes. She jumped into her Charger and I tried to follow, but her car was too fast. I lost her after two turns."

"Fuck," Dax said, his insides churning with rage. His heartbreak was long gone and the only thing left was pure determination. "Meet me back at the Void. It's time to go witch hunting."

Leo was silent as he stared at his mentor.

"There's no time for hesitation, Leo," Dax said. "We'll get Prim into custody at the office, but then we've got a job to do."

"Okay, Dax," Leo said, his expression grave.

"I don't like it any better than you do, kid," Dax said. "But this is the job. Get used to it." Even though Dax delivered his lines with no room for argument, he felt the words turn to ash on his tongue. It was true that sometimes agents went rogue, but it wasn't true that he could or should ever be okay with having to hunt his own girlfriend. With every muscle tensed with pure frustration, Dax returned to the Trooper and the shifter waiting for him.

"Is it true?" she asked, her eyes wide. "Did she really kill my cousin?"

Dax clenched the steering wheel and nodded once. There was nothing else to say.

LEO AND DAX spent the next three nights patrolling the rest of the Masterson pack. There were only four names on the list, but being in the same pack was their only connection. They were family and not much more. They didn't even hang out together unless it was a giant family gathering like a wedding or reunion.

Dax sat in his Trooper, eating a po'boy from a local neighborhood place, and suddenly stiffened. The hair stood up on the back of his neck, and he knew he was being watched. He sent a quick text to Leo. *Where are you?*

Uptown. Maci's parents are attending a charity ball.

Already? Dax thought. Their daughter's death had only been a week ago. It was hard to imagine them out at a charity ball. *I'm in Lakeview. I think something's about to go down.*

I'm on my way.

Dax shoved the phone into his pocket and jumped out of the Trooper. The street was darker than he remembered. He glanced up, noting the lack of the moon and the fact that the light was out in the nearby lamppost. It had been lit the night before. He remembered it illuminating the old VW Beetle still sitting in the same spot. Thick humidity clung to his skin, making it harder for him to breathe. It was the kind of night that was made for trouble.

The stillness unsettled him. He hadn't forgotten that someone was watching him, but who? Was it Phoebe? One of the pack members? A vampire? He didn't know. There wasn't anyone on the street. No one he could see anyway.

Dax pressed a hand to his belt, his fingers running over the hilt of the dagger he'd been wearing since he suspected Phoebe of going rogue. Three days ago, he'd added a tranq gun and a stun gun. He'd left his handgun in the safe. When the shit hit the fan, he didn't want to be the one pulling the trigger. Phoebe was dangerous, but he didn't want to see her dead. He wanted answers.

"Hello, Dax." Her rough voice floated through the thick air from somewhere behind him.

Dax's skin prickled. It looked like he was going to get those answers sooner rather than later. "Why'd you do it, Phoebe?"

"I'm not sure you really want to know." Her voice came from in front of him now even though he hadn't turned.

"Don't play games. It's not your style. Not with me anyway," he said, unable to keep the irritation out of his tone.

"You're right. I never did play games with you. But things are different now. You're the one standing in the way of what I want. So unless you hand over those two shifters you're protecting, the games are about to get real sporty."

"Stop fucking around, Phoebe. Just tell me why. The truth this time."

"I already told you. They killed my brother," she snarled. "All because he refused to do their bidding."

"That's a lie. Willow saw Seth just a few days ago," Dax said, scanning the area for any hint of the dark-haired beauty.

"So he's back here, is he? That figures. Even after eight years, he still doesn't give a shit about me."

Dax had no idea what she meant. At that moment, he really didn't care either. All he wanted to do was take her in and get her a psych evaluation, see if she'd suffered a major breakdown. To his uneducated eye, it sure seemed as if a switch had flipped that day she was supposed to leave the healer's office.

"Why do you say that?" he asked, just to keep her talking.

She snorted. "Because all he cares about is her, that's why."

"Who's her?"

Phoebe didn't answer.

Instead, he felt the first effects of a spell hurtling right toward him. "Fuck!" Dax threw himself to the ground, simultaneously shifting into his wolf form. It was his best shot at outrunning or surviving her spells. In his wolf form, he could shake off certain spells as well as move faster if he needed to dodge her wrath. His paws hit the pavement and he darted around a nearby 1950s-style truck, taking cover just before the magic hit the fender and sizzled all over the metal bodywork.

"Don't be afraid, Dax. I just want to go somewhere and talk. That wouldn't be so bad, would it?"

He let out a growl. If she really just wanted to talk, she wouldn't be throwing her magic around.

"I'm just trying to persuade you to see reason." Another bolt of magic flew right past him and blasted a chunk out of a nearby tree.

How? By taking off a limb? He darted under the truck and came out the other side, just in time to see her touch the ring on her index finger. *Sleeping potion.* As long as she hadn't changed the spell, she was intending to knock him out. That was better than the death curse, he supposed.

"Come on, Dax," she cooed. "It's just me and you now. You don't really think I'd hurt you, not after all the nights we've spent together?"

If he'd been in his human form, he would've snorted. Did she really think she could use their sex life to convince him to do anything? If he knew anything about Kilsen, it was that physical intimacy came easy to her. It was the emotional closeness that was deeper and meant something. If she was going to appeal to his sense of loyalty to her, that's where she should've been focusing her efforts. The fact that she wasn't was interesting.

He crept along the row of cars, circling back to where he'd left his clothes and personal items. He might be able to fend off a magical attack easier in his wolf form, but taking her down without ripping a limb off would be quite a bit harder.

"Come here, puppy," she sang, sounding like a lunatic.

His nostrils flared and for a second, he wasn't sure he was going to be able to shift. He was too angry. But then he saw his pile of clothes and the tranq gun. In an instant, he was back in human form. There was no time to get redressed. He just grabbed the tranq gun and fired.

Phoebe held up one hand, creating a magical shield of light that illuminated her dark expression. The dart lodged into her magical barrier and when she snapped her fingers, the dart fell to the ground. "That was... disappointing."

Dax gaped at her. He'd never seen her use such a spell before, and the brimstone scent in the air told him everything he needed to know about why. Brimstone was an illegal substance. Witches used it to enhance their powers, but it also messed up their brain chemistry.

Suddenly Dax felt sick. Was that why all this was happening? She'd poisoned herself with brimstone and had now gone off the deep end? "You don't have to do this, Phoebe. The Void is ready to help you through this. We'll get you a psych evaluation, and from there—"

"No! I will not be a prisoner again," she cried and threw

her hands up in the air. Raindrops so hot they burned fell from the sky and sizzled when they hit Dax's skin.

He hissed and dove for the stun gun, but Phoebe's foot hit the weapon just before his fingers closed over the metal case.

"Get up," she ordered, snapping her fingers and making the rain turn to tiny slivers of ice.

Dax immediately turned back into his wolf and roared at her, his jaws open, and then he pounced.

She pivoted quickly, her movements as graceful as a dancer's when she turned back toward him and reach out her left hand.

He took his shot and clamped his jaws around her wrist.

But instead of trying to get free, she just gave him a cat-that-ate-the-canary grin and said, "Good night, Dax. We'll talk in the morning."

Gold dust sprinkled down on him, pulling him into pure darkness.

Chapter Twenty-One

"Fuck," Dax whispered, taking a step away from me.

I turned around and met Allcot's caustic stare. "Hello, Eadric. I didn't think you'd be in tonight."

"I came to collect my wife. I see I shouldn't have bothered," he said, moving gracefully into the room, straight toward me.

"I'm sure Pandora would've come and gotten me."

"She's tending to Lex." His cold gaze landed on Dax. "I told you I'd end you if you ever touched her. Did I not?"

"You did," Dax agreed, standing his ground right next to me. "But it appears she isn't the property you thought she was."

A small cheer rose up in the back of my throat, but I swallowed it. Now wasn't the time. "Listen, Allcot," I started.

"Stop talking, Phoebe," he ordered and reached for Dax, grabbing him by the shirt and yanking the shifter toward him. "You, servant, are a dead man."

"Allcot!" I jumped between them, grabbing Eadric's wrist

and forcing him to let go of Dax's shirt. "You will not harm my oldest and dearest friend."

The chill of his gaze landed on me, and he let out a hiss that made my ears ring. "The only reason this loser isn't dead already is because I promised your brother I'd keep him alive. But you ruined that, didn't you, Phoebe? Once a whore, always a whore."

Oh, that was it. I'd had enough. "I was never a whore, you low-life, second-class vampire. I've seen you in your three-way sex-fests where all you care about is what pleasure your women can give you. I'll never understand how Pandora —" Shit. My anger had gotten the best of me, and I was giving him a dressing-down for the actions of the Allcot from my world, not this one. Not that I thought any better of him.

"Pandora?" he asked, showing the barest hint of interest. "Pandora and I..." He shook his head and narrowed his gaze. "What are you talking about?"

"Nothing. It was probably just a false memory or a dream or something," I said, again biting back a wince.

"No. I don't think so." He reached out and grabbed me by the neck, pushing me back toward the wall. "Explain yourself, Phoebe."

At least we were on solid footing now. I knew how to fight vampires, especially vampires who were pissed. I answered with a knee to the groin.

Allcot easily sidestepped my attack, but I'd known he would. I'd been here before. Maybe not with *this* Allcot, but one who moved in very much the same way. I countered by going for a knee. My foot hit the target, and I put everything I had into the blow. It knocked Allcot off-balance, causing him to topple to the side. He went down and started to roll, but Dax was on him, already in wolf form, his gray and white fur illuminated by the overhead light.

I ran around the pair, automatically reaching for the agate I kept in my pocket. My fingers came up empty as I remembered I hadn't had it on me the day I'd slipped into this other realm. "Dammit!" Instead, I reached for the dagger I had strapped to my leg and felt whole for the first time in days as my hand wrapped around the hilt.

Dax had wrapped his jaws around Allcot's shoulder and was hanging on with a fierce grip as he shook his head. It looked as if the wolf was trying to tear Allcot's arm right off. And why wouldn't he? The vampire had been prepared to keep Dax chained to this business for the rest of his life, and all because Dax had feelings for the wife Allcot had fucking purchased. The entire thing was so gross, it made my stomach turn just thinking about it.

Allcot got his other hand wrapped around Dax's furry neck, grabbed on, and threw the wolf so hard he hit the plaster wall and slid down in a heap of limbs and fur. Before I could even move, Allcot was on his feet and coming straight toward me.

Fine. I was ready. I kept a tight grip on the dagger's hilt and danced out of his way, anticipating which way he'd move before he even got there. Then I pivoted and landed the dagger right in the same shoulder that was now marred with puncture wounds from Dax's impressive canines.

"Fuuuuuuck!" Allcot roared, twisting and grabbing my wrist. His grip was so tight it caused me to release the hilt, leaving the dagger still sticking out of his shoulder. And that's when the blow came. His fist landed just to the left of my right eye, sending me spinning back. Pain exploded in my skull, and I felt as if my head had literally cracked in two.

It was my turn to go down in a pile of limbs, but as I did, I saw Dax going back for more, his lithe body leaping through the air and catching Allcot on the neck.

Good, I thought. Let's see how he likes it. Though judging by the grumbling coming from the salty vampire, I was guessing it wasn't a pleasurable experience. That was no surprise. Allcot understood pleasure. He understood bringing himself pleasure by belittling others. It was rare when he actually fought his own battles. Though I'd seen it before, seen him sacrifice himself for Pandora actually.

Dax went flying through the air a second time. I didn't hesitate—I grabbed my dagger, which had been thrown to the floor, and bounced back up on my feet, ready for him. But the vampire moved so fast I didn't even see him coming. The dagger was ripped from my hand and the next thing I knew, I was pressed up against the wall, Allcot at my back and his fangs at my neck.

"Now what's the plan, Phoebe," he hissed in my ear.

"I could still spell you," I said, running on pure adrenaline and bravado. If this were the Allcot I knew in my reality, I wouldn't be afraid of him. It was highly unlikely he'd kill the best friend of Willow Rhoswen. They had family connections now, not to mention Willow was a damned valuable fae to the vampire community. But in this reality? I likely wasn't valuable at all.

"With what? That death ring you're still wearing from last week that we had you spell just in case it was needed?" He ran his fingers down my throat as if searching for the best place to lodge his fangs.

"That's a possibility," I said and swallowed hard.

He pressed his body into me, letting me feel his arousal against my back. It made me shudder in disgust. Leave it to

Allcot to be turned on by violence. Not that I was surprised. It was a fairly typical response for vamps. "I'm already dead, remember?"

Of course I did. But it was likely potent enough to at least knock him out. "I remember."

There was a groan across the room, and I took that to mean that Dax had shifted back into his human form. That meant he was hurt and likely hadn't had a choice. Damn.

Allcot let out a growl of impatience as he ground his hips into me, but then he suddenly jerked back, letting me go.

I fell against the wall, stunned, unsure of what was happening. Slowly I turned around and faced him.

Those gray eyes were full of lust but also anger as he studied me. "Who are you?"

"What?" I gave my head a little shake, trying to follow his sudden pivot.

"You're not Phoebe Kilsen. I knew a week ago, but I bought your story about taking herbs." He scowled and glared at me. "You're someone else. The Phoebe I know doesn't fight like you do. She's dirtier, more vicious. Scrappy, like a street fighter. You… you've been trained." He walked over to his desk and leaned against it, his arms crossed over his chest. "Not to mention that the minute I pressed my dick into her ass, she would've crushed my balls. But twice you just stood there, seething while fear rolled off you. The Phoebe I know doesn't give a shit about what I do. She'd rather die fighting than let me see her afraid. Mind telling me where my wife is?"

"I wasn't afraid," I said, lifting my chin. Though I had been at least a little bit. I didn't know this vamp. Not this version of him anyway.

He snorted his derision. "You just keep telling yourself

that, honey." He glanced at Dax. "Did you know she's a fake?"

Dax, who had managed to get back into his jeans, walked over to me, placing a hand on the small of my back. "No," he finally said, not looking at me. "But it makes sense. She's softer. More heart."

"I'm not soft," I insisted.

Both of the men just stared at me, saying nothing. But then Dax cleared his throat. "I see you aren't denying it."

"Dammit." I stalked over to the velvet couch and sat down, impressed with Allcot. He was still a dick, just like he was in my world, but he was smart. He was also complicated, with many layers. His ethics were problematic as usual, but when he cared about someone, he was loyal. Even to my counterpart, who had bailed on him. "Listen, I'm not crazy, okay?"

"Okay," Dax said, taking the seat next to me. Allcot stayed where he was, a stormy expression on his face.

"I'm from a parallel universe," I blurted. "I *am* Phoebe Kilsen, just not the one you two have known all these years."

Allcot blinked at me.

Dax studied my face as if he was seeing me for the first time.

"That's not possible," Allcot finally said.

I shrugged. "That's what I said. Then I ended up slipping through some portal and your wife took my spot in my realm. Trust me when I tell you I'm not happy about it."

"But the portals have been sealed," Allcot insisted.

It was my turn to blink. "You knew there were parallel universes?" I asked, shocked. Though I don't know why I should've been. If anyone knew about the portals, it would be

Allcot. He was a resourceful bastard. It would serve me well to remember that.

"Of course I knew. Shifters from the Masterson clan opened them to escape their death sentence after they killed Phoebe's brother."

Holy shit. He knew about Seth. "So you know then. About Seth."

"I know," he said.

"How? Were you around when he died?" I asked, wanting to know how much he knew about the portals.

"My wife told me. She tells me everything. That's why this week has been so... challenging." He pushed himself up from the desk and said, "You should've just been up front with me from the beginning. It would've made everything easier."

"Seth said... Never mind. I just didn't think it was safe to start talking about parallel universes. One never knows how people are going to take those things."

Allcot studied me and then gave me a quick nod as if to say he understood my position. But then he pivoted when he said, "Phoebe will be back. When she's done with her business, she'll come home to me." His gaze moved to Dax's guarded one. "You won't be here when she does."

A shiver went up my spine at the look Allcot gave him. It was full of venom and jealousy.

"Dax didn't do anything wrong," I insisted. "In fact, you probably owe him your gratitude."

"Phoebe," Dax said, shaking his head.

"No, Dax, he needs to hear this." I stalked over to Allcot and stood right in front of him. "Did you know he gave up his freedom to watch over her eight years ago?"

Allcot cut his gaze to the shifter, but only briefly. He didn't answer.

"I'll take that as a no."

"I guess that means you also don't know that Phoebe's brother, the one who died, also promised to come back here with enough cash to free both Phoebe and Dax. And then four years later, you stroll in and purchase her freedom, but no one did anything for Dax here. And to make matters worse, you were just going to let him rot here, bound to this place forever. That's… it's fucking cruel, Allcot. You know that?"

His lips twitched into that sinister smile he wore when he was amused by something. "The shifter is right. You are softer."

"Fuck you," I said and met his steely gaze with one of my own.

"Yeah, you are. You care too much." The vampire took a step forward and placed his large hands on my shoulders. Then he did the oddest thing. He lowered his head and kissed me on the forehead. "You and I would've been a terrible match. At least I understand your demand for new contracts now." He let out a small snort. "And the reason you were locking lips with that one." He jerked his head in Dax's direction. "I bet he's a lot like the Dax in your reality."

I turned my attention to the shifter in question and sighed. "Yeah, he is. This one has a bigger hero complex though."

"Hey, I'm sitting right here," Dax said.

I chuckled. "Don't worry. It's pretty endearing."

"Listen, Phoebe. I'll make you a deal," Allcot said.

I stiffened. "About what?"

"I'll let the shifter go free, no strings attached, if you tell me about Eadric Allcot in your realm."

Dax sat up straighter, interest lighting his handsome face.

Sighing, I closed my eyes and wondered if this was a good idea. Allcot was a big-ass deal in my reality. Would that give this one ideas or make him want to try to find a way into the other realm? I didn't see how he could though, unless he found a way to get the other Allcot to cross over. If he was stuck here, what was the harm in a little information? The sinking feeling in the pit of my stomach told me I should keep my mouth shut. Or at least say as little as possible. But when I glanced at Dax again, all I saw was a good man who was just on the other line of absolute freedom, and I knew I was going to say yes. But first there had to be a negotiation.

"All right. I'm inclined to tell you what you want to know, but I need a few things first."

Allcot let out a loud laugh. "Of course you do. Fine. Name your terms."

"A bonus for Dax because he kept an eye on Phoebe for four years. Enough that it equals pay for the eight years that he worked here. Bouncer wages."

"What else?" he asked.

"Willow gets her bonus early and doesn't have to work here anymore. I know there's a new one-year contract, but I want her out of here and going to culinary school full-time."

"Fine. Done," Allcot said as if he didn't have to even think about it.

"There's one more thing," I said.

"Of course there is," Allcot muttered. "There's always something."

I ignored his snark and tried to sort out what I wanted to say. This was a tricky one and I started to sweat, wondering if I would go to hell for making the request. Seth would probably like to send me there. But everything in me told me he could not stay in this reality. That Allcot would burn him when Allcot and Pandora ended up together somehow. I sucked in a sharp breath and said, "After your Phoebe comes back and I leave here, I assume you'll be finding a way to reseal those portals, right?"

"Yes. It's dangerous to leave them open. Anyone or anything can crawl through," he said, giving me the side-eye.

"Right. Okay then. I need you to make sure Seth and Heather, your employee from Baton Rouge, cross back into my realm before you reseal the portals. They both belong in my reality."

Surprise lit Allcot's once-passive face. "You want Seth to leave his son?"

"No," I said with a squeak. "But when I fill you in on the details of your other life, you're going to understand why I'm asking for this."

He leaned forward just enough to invade my personal space and offered me his hand. "I think we have a deal, Kilsen."

Nausea roiled in my gut, but I placed my hand in his, closed my eyes, and tried to pretend I hadn't just made a deal with the devil.

Chapter Twenty-Two

"ood morning." Phoebe's voice was the first thing Dax heard when he woke from his dreamless slumber.

He blinked, clearing the sleep from his vision. She was standing in the doorway, holding a mug with both hands, smiling at him. Warmth filled all his empty spaces, and he smiled back. "Morning, gorgeous."

"It's about time you woke up. I was starting to think my sleeping spell had malfunctioned. And you're no use to me incapacitated."

"What?" He tried to scramble into a sitting position, but as soon as he moved, he heard the clink of chains and was thwarted by his restraints. He glanced down the length of his naked body, noting the shackles at his feet. Groaning, he glanced from side to side and grimaced at the matching restraints around his wrists.

Fuck me, he thought. He hadn't woken in her bed, and it hadn't all just been a nightmare.

"Sorry about that," she said sweetly, sitting in a wooden

chair right next to the bed. "I couldn't have you running off before we had our chat." The aroma of coffee filled the room, and when she saw Dax staring at the mug, she took a slow sip, never breaking eye contact. "I'll get you some if you call into the Void and have them release those two shifters."

"Forget it," he growled.

She shrugged. "Suit yourself."

He glanced around at the barren room. The gray walls were void of any decoration, while the bed and chair were the only two pieces of furniture. There wasn't even a window. "Where are we?"

"Does it matter?" She got up and moved back to the door. "I'll tell you when you've given me what I need."

"What's that, Phoebe?" he ground out.

"The freedom to settle the score." She disappeared, leaving him alone on the double bed and struggling to pull the restraints from the wall.

When it became clear the restraints weren't budging, he closed his eyes and willed himself to shift.

Nothing happened.

He tried again, felt the pull in his belly, but just lay there panting. He closed his eyes and let out a frustrated growl. She'd spelled the restraints. It was the only way his shift could be blocked. Hatred rose up from deep in his gut, and he started to wonder how he'd never seen this side of Phoebe before. He was also pissed at himself for getting into this position. He should've known better. Should've realized she'd stop at nothing to get what she wanted. But he'd be damned if he gave in. She'd have to kill him first.

Dax lay there, staring at the ceiling for what seemed like hours, replaying the events of the evening, berating himself for falling victim to Phoebe, all the while knowing he couldn't have seen the brimstone angle coming. In the time that he'd known her, she'd never used forbidden magic. It hadn't occurred to him that she would now. He wasn't sure how long he lay there, listening to the settling of the house and Phoebe's footsteps, wondering when she was going to finally grace him with her presence again.

Sleep took him again, and this time when he woke, Phoebe was standing over him, holding a tray of food. "Sit up."

He tested his restraints and realized they'd been loosened enough to let him prop himself up against the headboard. After he pushed himself up, she set the tray over his lap. Eggs, bacon, and toast were on a paper plate and steaming coffee filled a paper cup. No utensils. He didn't care. His stomach rumbled with hunger, and he finished off the food in record time. Once the plate was empty, Phoebe handed him a paper napkin.

"Now that you've been fed, I hope you've decided to be helpful."

"Why are you doing this?" he asked, his eyes narrowed. "What did those shifters do to send you over the edge."

"I *told* you. They killed my brother."

"No. They didn't. He was spotted looking for you just a few days ago," Dax said carefully.

"Yeah, so he can force me back into the clutches of Allcot," she said with so much derision that she actually shook.

Allcot? He stared at her with curious confusion. "What do you mean?"

She fisted her hand in her hair and started to pace. "It's his idea of a *better* life. His way of saving me from a life of indentured servitude. Only I traded one master for another. I'm done, understand? Done."

She was mad. He was sure of it. Nothing she said made sense. Seth dead? A servant to Allcot? Neither was true. And she thought the shifters had killed her brother. She needed help. Maybe he could convince her he'd help, get her to undo his restraints. If he went along with her story, pretended to believe her, she might start to trust him. He didn't have anything to lose.

"Sure. No one wants to be under Allcot's thumb. I can see why that wouldn't sit well with you. What does he want you to do?"

She snorted. "Have his child. There's no way in hell I'm carrying his offspring. He thinks I want to. I've made sure of that. It's the only way to survive that nightmare. But that's over. I'm tired of making him feel like he's the center of my world. He's not and never has been."

Dax blinked. That was impossible. Vampires couldn't father children. "That's… quite the ask. How does Pandora feel about it?"

"She thinks it's great. Then Lex would have a cousin. But then I'd never get away from that controlling asshole. I can't let my brother's imposter take me back. All he cares about is his actual sister. Not this fake one. I'm sure he's only here to get me to help her. Well, she can have Allcot's bastard. If being his wife was good enough for me, it's good enough for her."

Dax's heart rose up and got caught in his throat. *All he cares about is his actual sister? Not this fake one?* Was she saying she wasn't Dax's Phoebe? She was his Phoebe's double? A doppelgänger of sorts? "You said Seth only cares about his actual sister. Where is she?"

"Not here." The fake Phoebe laughed. "And she never will be if I have anything to say about it. In this world, Allcot is with Pandora. He doesn't want me. I'm free. But first I have to take out the shifters who killed my brother. That's it, then I'll leave you all alone."

"In this world?" Dax asked. "What does that mean exactly?"

She sucked in a sharp breath. "What do you think it means? Don't be dense, Dax. You really think there's only one world, one timeline, one reality?"

A sinking feeling materialized in his gut as he started to understand what she was talking about. "You're saying there's an alternate universe and that the Phoebe I know is there while you're here, settling some score? Is that it?"

She gave him a slow smile. "That's right, Dax. You're just as smart in this world as you are in mine. I'm glad to see it. I hope that means you'll get with the program sooner rather than later."

He felt sick. She'd either gone insane from the brimstone or his Phoebe was stuck in another universe. He vehemently hoped for the latter even if it did sound crazy.

"What do you say, Dax? Are you ready to call off the dogs?"

He swallowed hard, trying to wrap his head around her revelation. It certainly would explain a lot. "Are Prim Masterson and Lincoln Frost from your reality?"

"Of course they are," she said, giving him a look of pure disbelief. "Why else would I target them?"

"Okay." He blew out a long breath, having trouble picturing Maci Masterson as a cold-blooded killer. But he hadn't met her in person, had he? He'd only talked to her friends and family. "Is the entire Masterson pack from your reality?"

She shook her head. "No. Just the four of them. To make a long story short, Maci came through first after her doppelgänger had a freak accident. She picked off the other three so her gang could follow. Once they were here, they slipped into their doppelgänger's roles and carried on as if they hadn't just taken over someone else's lives. They're disgusting, horrible people, especially Maci. I'm glad I found that bitch first. She's the one who took my brother down. They were dating, and she turned out to be a real black widow type."

Dax just blinked at her. Her story seemed so fantastical, and yet... he felt like it was the first time she'd been truthful with him in days.

"So, big guy. Are you going to pull through and help me out, or am I going to have to twist your arm?" She gave him a wicked little smile and scanned his body with her hungry gaze. "My Dax always did like it when I got a little rough with him."

"Your Dax? You mean my doppelgänger in your world?"

She nodded. "The one and only. It's a well-known fact that parallel worlds mirror each other. Dax Marrok is the only person I'll miss. But knowing him, he'll just be glad I'm finally away from Allcot. Free for the first time in eight years."

Dax was stunned, overwhelmed by the information she'd just dumped on him. It was a lot to process, but mostly he was just surprised that he believed her. She was coherent, and her words had the ring of honesty. But that still didn't mean he could turn two shifters loose for her to exact her revenge. If they had killed her brother, they should stand trial. "Don't you think it would be better to let the law take care of Prim and Lincoln? We already have them in custody."

She raised one eyebrow. "My experience with the law is less than encouraging."

"I'm the law," Dax said, realizing she hadn't gone into detail about the specifics of the world she was from, but it sounded oppressive… for her at least.

"I won't negotiate, Dax. It doesn't matter how many of those imploring looks you give me. I've seen too much. Release them and I'll let you go. You'll never have to see me again." She crossed her arms over her chest and stared him down.

"What about my Phoebe?" he asked.

She shrugged. "She stepped into my world. Don't ask me how. That's not how it's supposed to work. Doppelgängers aren't supposed to be able to occupy the same world. But she did, and that's not my fault. I saw my chance and took it. I won't go back. Besides, I don't even know if I could go back. Not unless she dies anyway."

Dax felt the blood drain from his face.

"I'm sorry. But like I said, the two worlds do mirror each other. It seems as if being separated from the one you love is in the cards."

He wouldn't accept that. He couldn't. If the Seth that was roaming this world was her actual brother, he knew the pair of them could team up and force this Phoebe back into her world and bring his back. But first he had to get out of those damned restraints. He stared her directly in the eye. "Let me free and I'll help you."

The faux Phoebe narrowed her eyes at him. "How can I trust you?"

"Do you trust the Dax in your world?"

"Yes." The response was instantaneous.

"Then there's your answer."

She seemed to contemplate his response for a long moment. Then she gave him a curt nod and said, "Don't double-cross me. Trust me when I say that just because you look like the one person I've ever loved, it won't stop me from doing what I have to do."

"You mean you'll kill me too?" he asked, raising one eyebrow.

She gave him a slow nod. "I won't want to, but I will."

He stared at her determined expression, the one he knew so well, and understood that she was telling the truth. This would be war, and he was going to have to be prepared for it. "All right. Let me go and I'll make the call."

Chapter Twenty-Three

I sat at the dinner table at Allcot's plantation home and watched as Allcot eyed Pandora. I'd noticed before the way he stared at her, but now it looked a lot more like raw hunger. My gut was a mess. I'd told Allcot everything. How he was the most powerful vampire in the city. That Pandora was his consort and they were madly in love. That he'd turned her years ago. That he had an adopted son named David. And that I'd never met a Lex.

Where did Seth's little boy fit in the parallel universe order?

Allcot speculated that there was only one. That because Seth had hopped universes, there was no way for him to exist in both realities.

The theory made sense. I just didn't know if that meant that the kid could hop between the two or not. I guessed yes. He had no double keeping him stuck in one place. But if Seth took him back to our world, it would mean taking him away from his mother. And if I knew Seth, he'd never do that.

My head started to throb. What had I done? Allcot was

now openly coveting Pandora. And she was smiling at him as if she was eating it up. She didn't even glance in my direction once to see if I cared.

I didn't, not for myself anyway, but I did feel bad for Seth. I'd walked into his reality and completely fucked up his life. Of course, an argument could be made that because he hadn't been honest with me, he'd fucked up mine, but it wasn't the same, and I knew it. He hadn't actively tried to keep me away from the one person I loved most in the world.

Dammit! I pushed away from the table, no longer caring about food. Instead, I climbed the stairs and found my way into Lex's room. The young boy was sitting in the middle of his bed, playing with a stuffed dog and a small green tank. The dog was riding on top, literally barking orders to the tank operator.

"Hey, cutie pie. Mind if I join you?" I asked from the doorway.

Lex looked up and grinned. "Hi, Auntie Phoebe. There's another puppy right there." He pointed to a larger stuffed dog that had zero chance of fitting on top of his tank.

I strolled in and sat cross-legged on his bed, holding the puppy and chiming in with barks here and there as Lex revved the engine and made squealing sounds, indicating the vehicle was rounding corners.

We sat there together, innocently playing until Lex's eyes got droopy and he let out a giant yawn.

"Hey, little buddy. Looks like you're getting tired. Wanna lie down? I'll read you a story."

He nodded, pulled back the covers, and climbed in. I positioned myself beside him and draped an arm around him, cuddling him close as I read him a book about a talking alligator. He knew all the words and recited them with me, his gentle voice both soothing and breaking my heart at the same time.

When the little boy's breathing turned heavy with sleep, I slipped off the bed, tucked him in, and tiptoed out into the hall. Normally I'd retreat to my studio and hide out for the rest of the evening. But after spending the past hour holding my nephew, I knew there was something I had to rectify. I couldn't let Allcot kick Seth back into his realm. Not when his son was here. I'd been out of my mind to suggest such a thing.

I still believed that this world would break Seth's heart in many ways, but those were his choices to make. Not mine. Steeling myself, I descended the stairs, prepared to retract the final demand I'd made Allcot agree to in exchange for knowledge. I'd leave it up to Seth to decide.

The grand staircase creaked under the weight of my feet as I made it back down to the first floor. Everything else was silent, as if I were the only person in the house. But I knew that wasn't the case. I'd left Allcot and Pandora at the kitchen table when I'd bolted, unable to stomach their blatant attraction.

I wondered if Seth ever saw it. If he did, I suppose he just looked the other way. He knew as well as I did that the two had something explosive in our own world. The fact that he'd chosen to marry her anyway was a puzzle. I hadn't thought to ask. Of course, I'd been worried about other things since arriving, and his business was his business.

I just wish I'd thought of that before I'd stuck my big nose in the middle of his life. I rounded the corner and made my way down to Allcot's study. I was about to knock when I thought I heard a crash and a woman let out a cry of distress.

What the fuck? My fight reflex kicked in, and I burst

through the door, ready to kick some ass. Only the minute I stepped into the room, I froze and stared in complete shock at the scene in front of me.

Allcot's bare ass was right there in front of my face, pumping frantically away as he fucked Pandora on top of his desk. Her legs were wrapped around his hips and her head was thrown back in ecstasy as he drank from her neck, both of them moaning their pleasure and completely unaware they had an audience.

Slowly I backed out of the room and very carefully closed the door, holding my breath until I heard the tiny click of the latch. Then I ran upstairs, praying they hadn't noticed me.

Chapter Twenty-Four

*D*ax had been planning on calling Leo, to somehow code his message so that the kid realized the two shifters needed to be followed.

But the faux Phoebe was way ahead of him. She dialed the director instead. After handing him the phone, she whispered, "Just tell her you have Phoebe in custody and that the shifters are free to go."

Dax ground his teeth together. It was sort of true. He did have the faux Phoebe. He didn't exactly have control over her though. And if what she said was true, there was no way in hell those two shifters should walk. But he argued with himself that they'd been model citizens over the past eight years. It didn't excuse anything, but they could always pick them up again, right? He cleared his throat. "Director Halston. It's Marrok…"

"Agent Marrok. I've been expecting your call. Is everything under control? Have you found Kilsen yet?

"Yes, fine. Phoebe's here. I'm getting ready to bring her

in, and you can go ahead and let Prim and Lincoln go. They're safe now."

Silence.

"Director?"

No response.

He pulled the smart phone away from his ear and noted the call had ended. But instead of reacting, he just nodded at the faux Phoebe and pressed the phone back to his ear. "There you are. You cut out for a moment. ... Yes. It's all under control. ... Yes, there's a really good explanation. I'll put it in the report. ... Thank you, Director." Dax pressed his finger to the space where the call would end and handed the phone back to Phoebe.

She shoved it into her back pocket and nodded to the bed. "Get back on the mattress. I need a head start, and the only way to get that is to restrain you again."

No fucking way. Dax stood rooted to the floor, watching her, wondering what she was going to do when she realized he'd refused. Another sleeping spell? He glanced at her ring, the one that he knew contained the sleeping dust.

"Dax," she warned.

"Phoebe." He lunged, going straight for the ring. Electric magic streamed from her hand, and it was then he noticed he was holding a metal amulet of sorts. Before, he'd thought it was her agate. No wonder the magic was different. The thought whirled through his head as he threw himself to the floor and came up, rolling back on his feet. But her magic hit him right in the chest, sending a ripple of electricity straight through him. His body twitched from the magic, but he found he was unable to force himself to move while he waited for the magic to burn itself out.

"It would've hurt less and been much easier if you'd have

just done what I asked," she said with a *tsk* and pushed him over.

He fell half on the bed and half off, but that was no problem for the faux Phoebe. She clamped his wrists and ankles back into their restraints and then tugged on some sort of pulley system until he was back in the middle of the mattress, completely incapacitated.

"You bitch," he muttered, hating her and hating himself for not being able to outmatch a witch. He'd always known his Phoebe would likely kick his ass in a fight, but now he knew for sure. Her magic was just too powerful. That made her a great partner, but it sucked when she turned her wrath on him.

"Sorry, puppy," she said with a saccharine smile. "But I'll be out of your hair soon."

"I don't think so," a vaguely familiar male voice said, followed by a flash of pure white magic.

Phoebe pivoted quickly, and Dax noted the scowl just before she flashed her metal amulet. Their two streams of magic collided, sparking like fireworks on the Fourth of July.

The male witch came into view, and Dax recognized him. Seth, Phoebe's brother, stood there, magic pouring from the hilt of a dagger. It was remarkably similar to the one that Phoebe usually carried.

"Stop this, Phoebs," Seth ordered. "It's time to go home."

"Stop trying to control me, you fucking bastard. Between you and Allcot, my life has been shit these past years. I'm not going anywhere with you."

"You don't mean that," he said, shaking his head and matching her flow of magic with ease. "You and Allcot have something. I've seen it."

She scoffed. "You've seen what I want you to see. Now

fuck off. I'm going after the last two shifters that killed my real brother. You can either help or get flattened when I steamroll you."

He seemed surprised by her revelation. Then his eyes narrowed. "What about Dax? You're just going to leave him there in Allcot's club, under his thumb?"

His words caused her to falter for just a second as she said, "He doesn't work for Allcot. He works for Clio."

Dax, unable to do anything but just listen in awe to the two of them spar, tried to make sense of what they were talking about. They were obviously talking about her Dax in the parallel universe. This Phoebe had said he was the only one she'd ever loved. But apparently not enough to go back. It surprised him that her rejection hurt him a little. She was the faux Phoebe. Not his Phoebe. It shouldn't matter who she decided to spend her life with as long as his Phoebe came back to him.

Seth's lips turned up into a fake smile. "Not anymore. He finally went in and took over… for you, I might add. Clio's dead."

She lowered her amulet and gaped at him. "Dax is bound to Allcot now?"

"Yes. Also because of you." He moved in closer, reaching a hand out as if to comfort her.

But the faux Phoebe jerked back, tears streaming down her face, and then twirled, using both hands to knock him upside the head.

Seth was thrown halfway across the room, and Phoebe ran out but was stopped when another witch pushed her back into the room.

Nicola, Pandora's half sister, filled the doorway and said, "Where are you headed, Phoebs?"

"Get the fuck out of my way." Phoebe tried to barrel past her, but Nicola raised one hand, creating an impressive clear barrier.

"I don't think so. No one wants trouble in this town," Nicola said. "Why don't you go back to where you came from and let us have Kilsen back?"

"Fuck off." The faux Phoebe threw her amulet at the barrier, causing it to shatter on impact. Then she ran. But Nicola was too quick. She reached out and grabbed faux Phoebe by the hair and jerked her back. The women fell to the hardwood floor, magic and arms and legs flailing.

Streams of pure electric magic bounced around the room, some of them hitting Dax and making him seize from the sheer intensity of it. He wasn't sure, but he thought Seth was suffering the same fate.

Then the bolts of lightning stopped, and Dax peered over the edge of the bed to find faux Phoebe sitting on top of Nicola, her hands around the other woman's neck, choking the life out of her.

"Phoebe," Dax shouted. "Stop! You're killing her."

But the crazed witch either didn't hear him or didn't care, because she only redoubled her efforts and started to pound Nicola's head against the floorboards, causing a sickening crunch to ring in Dax's ears.

"Jesus fuck," Dax said, pulling with everything he had against his restraints.

Nicola was going to die. Phoebe—the imposter—was going to kill her while Seth lay unconscious across the room and Dax watched helplessly from the bed.

"Nooooo!"

A warrior cry filled Dax's ears, and just as he lifted his gaze, he spotted Leo charging into the room, Seth's dagger in his fist, and before faux Phoebe could disentangle from Nicola, the knife plunged straight into Phoebe's back.

The woman's mouth dropped open, and instead of sound, only blood spilled out. She slumped over to the side, her entire body going limp.

Nicola sputtered and gasped for air as Leo dropped the dagger and sat back on his heels, his face completely white as he muttered over and over again, "I killed her. I killed Phoebe. Oh God, Dax, I killed her."

"Get me out of these restraints," Dax ordered.

Leo just blinked up at him, seemingly unable to process anything.

"Leo," Dax snapped. "Get on your feet. Release me from this bed. Now!" he roared.

The yelling seemed to snap the younger shifter out of his stupor because he finally jumped to his feet and surveyed Dax's predicament. "Sorry, Dax," the shifter said, his voice so low Dax barely heard him. "Those require magic."

"Fuck me."

"I've got it," Nicola croaked. She was upright and her neck was bright red, but she was very much alive. Unlike Phoebe, who appeared to be bleeding out all over the floor. With just one touch, the restraints disappeared and Dax scrambled off the bed, going straight to Phoebe.

There was excessive blood, but when he bent his face down to hers, she stared into his eyes and said, "Make those shifters pay." Then she passed out.

"Call an ambulance," Dax ordered. "Do it now."

Leo scrambled to his feet, breathing hard, and a moment later Dax heard the young shifter speak into the phone.

Nicola moved to hover over Phoebe. She took one look at the wound and cursed as she pressed her hand to the injury.

A pale yellow glow of magic lit Phoebe's skin. The wounded witch jerked as if she'd been shocked but then stilled as the bleeding stopped.

"What did you do?" Dax asked.

"Just stopped the bleeding with a little cauterization. It's going to leave a nasty scar, but it might save her life."

"Thanks," Dax said. He was already convinced that this Phoebe wasn't his Phoebe. She didn't fight like his Phoebe, and after listening to the words she'd had with Seth, he fully believed she was who she said she was. That didn't mean he wanted her to die. Nor did he want that on Leo's conscience.

Seth finally roused from his spot on the other side of the room. "Shit. What happened?"

"Your sister kicked your ass," Dax said.

"She's not my sister," Seth said automatically.

"I gathered that." Dax sucked in a deep breath. "I think it's time someone explained exactly what's going on."

Seth ran a hand over his thick dark locks and started with, "I've been living in an alternate universe for most of the past eight years. A week ago, my real sister and the Phoebe you all know and love, somehow walked through that portal and was stuck when her doppelgänger slipped through to this world, trapping her there."

Chapter Twenty-Five

"It looks like she'll live," Healer Imogen said.

Dax eyed the imposter Phoebe through a two-way mirror. The witch was sitting up, eating a sandwich. One would never guess that she'd almost died the day before. Dax turned to the healer. "Your work is impressive."

"Nicola deserves the credit," she said. "Her quick thinking saved the day."

"You're right about that." Dax glanced over his shoulder at the witch in question. She gave him a smirk and shrugged one shoulder as if to say it was no big deal. All in a day's work. "Is she ready to travel?"

"How far?" Imogen asked.

"Just out to River Road. Seth is ready to take her back home."

"Sure." She looked over at Phoebe's brother. "How are you? Head okay? That was some hit you took."

"Fine," he muttered.

"All right then." Imogen patted Dax on the arm. "When my favorite witch pops back in, make sure she comes to see me. I want to check her over again, just to be on the safe side."

"Will do," Dax said. Then he turned and left, heading straight for the director's office.

"MARROK, THERE YOU ARE." Director Halston had her gray hair pulled back into a long braid and was holding a thick file folder. "I've gone over everything you've reported, and the Void has decided to hold Prim Masterson and Lincoln Frost indefinitely."

Dax nodded. "Good. Do you need any testimony from… anyone before we make the switch?"

"No, we have everything we need. But I wanted to go over the story the Void is leaking today. Make sure Kilsen is filled in as soon as possible."

"What story?" Dax asked.

She held up the city newspaper. The headline read: ROGUE ARCANE AGENT GOES ON KILLING SPREE. There was a picture of Phoebe right beneath the headline.

Dax winced. "That's going to sting."

"Hopefully not too badly," the director said, giving Dax the closest thing to a sympathetic smile he'd ever seen on her face. "The Void directors have come up with an explanation for why it looks like one our best snapped. The story is Phoebe had a twin who had a psychotic break. She's the one who caused all the havoc while holding Phoebe prisoner in that run-down shack out in the bayou."

"Phoebe's going to hate that story," Dax said.

"Can you think of a better one? There's film of Kilsen fighting you, for fuck's sake."

The truth? Dax thought but didn't say it. He knew why they were going with a lie, and he couldn't even say he blamed them. The story was as close to the truth as they could get in any case. They didn't want to tell the public there was an alternate universe with parallel lives. It invited far too much curiosity. The Void didn't want to be responsible for two hundred people constantly trying to escape this reality for a new one. One that apparently was even worse than the one they lived in where Allcot ruled the city and occasional shifter wars broke out.

"Nah," Dax said, finally answering her question. He shook his head. The story sure as hell was better than the city thinking Phoebe was awaiting trial and then letting her off with all charges dropped. That had been the other idea. Phoebe didn't need the suspicion hanging around her neck. "Seems plausible enough as long as records of her show up in databases. The press will look."

"Good. We've already got someone dealing with the tech trail. Now go make the swap. I'd really like to see Kilsen again." She gave Dax a short, quick nod, dismissing him.

When Dax made it back to faux Phoebe's holding cell, Leo was in the room, watching her through the two-way mirror.

"Hey, man," Dax said, sitting down next to him. "How are you feeling today?"

"Sick to my stomach," he said, and judging by the green tinge of his skin, Dax had to conclude he was telling the truth.

"Eat something bad?" Dax asked, trying to keep it light.

"Haven't eaten since yesterday morning," the shifter confessed.

"You don't think that's half the problem?"

"Dax…" He closed his eyes and clutched his hair, pulling slightly. "I can't unsee what happened. I almost killed Phoebe."

"Not Phoebe," Dax insisted. "Her doppelgänger. And you did what you had to do. She was going to kill Nicola."

"I know," Leo said.

"No, I don't think you do." Dax tugged the kid to the back of the room so he was no longer staring at the faux Phoebe. "You're a hero, Leo. Without you, this all would've gone down much differently. Instead, everyone is safe, and we're headed out to make the exchange for Phoebs. Being a Void agent is often about making the tough choices. You don't need to feel bad about doing your job."

"I don't, I just…" He shrugged. "The idea that I could stab anyone, much less Phoebe, like that… It unsettled me, man. How do you deal?"

Dax peered at the kid. "You've been in fights before. Killed before too. That never seemed to bother you. Not like this. What is it, Leo?"

He bit down hard on his lip. And when he spoke, it was in the barest of whispers. "I felt like I was killing my own mother."

Oh hell, Dax thought to himself. His confession made perfect sense. Phoebe was his mother figure. Not nearly old enough, but the one who'd been watching over him the past year, through the death of his girlfriend and his stint with drugs. She'd been by his side every step of the way. Not knowing what to say, Dax just wrapped his arms around the kid and held on tight.

It took Leo a moment, but eventually the tension eased from his shoulders and he hugged Dax back. "Thanks, man," Leo said when they broke apart.

"She loves you too, you know." Dax winked at the young shifter. "You just wait until she hears what a hero you were. Talk about smothering. You're gonna want to throw her out after half a day, so hold on to the appreciation you have right now, huh, Leo?"

"I'm holding on," Leo said.

"Good. Let's go get my girl."

"THIS IS WHERE SHE LEFT US?" Leo blurted out as Seth directed them to the dilapidated old plantation. "You're kidding me."

"No, why?" Seth asked.

Dax and Leo shared a knowing glance before Dax said, "We actually ended up here while we were looking for her. I had a tip that she came out here looking for you. Someone spotted you, did you know that?"

"What?" Seth asked. "How? I was in the other reality."

Dax shrugged. "No idea, but someone peeped you apparently. Anyway, we were searching for her, and this shitty road just felt like it had her energy, so we turned down it and ended up at this house."

"I found her locket," Leo said. "We were going to keep searching, but then we got a text that Phoebe was spotted at Howler's, and we took off."

"So close and yet so far," faux Phoebe muttered from the back seat.

Dax glanced in the rearview mirror and said, "We know how you ended up in this world, but what did you do once you got here? How did you know where Phoebe's houses were or where to go?"

"Jesus." The surly witch rolled her eyes. "I had her car, which had her keys and wallet. Her address was right there on her license. And once I searched her room and found her lockbox—which was locked using fingerprint entry, thank you very much—I had everything I needed. Money... well, until it ran out. You should tell her to keep a bigger stash. And she had those addresses to her safe houses in there. Not just the addresses, but the real estate transactions. That was super helpful. I just hadn't counted on Dax being able to get in. Talk about sloppy. That's not how I'd do it."

"And how's that?" Leo asked dryly, clearly over feeling responsible about stabbing her through the lung.

"Never let a man have the keys to the kingdom. What else?" she replied.

Seth chuckled. "Yep, that's how she plays."

"Damned straight."

"Except for when it comes to Dax," Seth added. "No matter what she says, he's her weakness."

Dax didn't know how to respond to any of their conversation. He knew they were talking about the other Dax, but it still felt really strange.

"Yeah, well," faux Phoebe said. "Yours is Heather."

Seth's eyes darkened and he scowled at her. "Leave her out of this."

"Why? It's the truth." She shrugged and stared out the window at the old house.

"Ready?" Dax asked.

Faux Phoebe didn't budge as the rest of them climbed out of the Trooper.

Seth moved to her side of the vehicle and held the door open for her. "You don't want us to drag you out, do you?"

"You wouldn't dare," she said with a low snarl.

"Wouldn't I?" He glared back. "This exchange was ordered by the Void. Do you really think they're just going let one of their agents rot in the otherworld? They'll hunt you down and throw you back through in a potato sack if you don't cooperate. And think of what Allcot will have to say about that."

"Oh, shut the fuck up." She hauled herself out of the Trooper and, without another word, walked toward the house and disappeared into thin air.

Immediately the real Phoebe appeared. Her eyes immediately locked on Dax's and she ran, throwing herself into his arms.

Chapter Twenty-Six

I'd known they were there. It was as if I could feel Dax just waiting for me. My Dax, not the one in the alternate reality. The faux Dax, as I'd taken to calling him, had already received his back pay and had taken off to Baton Rouge to start fresh in a new city. I'd wanted to tell him to not give up on his Phoebe, but I'd already made enough of a mess of things. If those two had the will to work it out, they would. If they didn't, well, that was their business.

But as the hopeless romantic that I apparently was, I kinda thought they had a thing or two going for them. Faux Dax was now free and so was Phoebe. Or she would be if she decided to pursue the information I'd left for her in her witch basket up in her studio. After I'd been scandalized by Pandora and Allcot going at it in his office, I'd run back up to the room I'd been staying in and wrote a long letter to my doppelgänger.

I told her everything from where she might find Dax and Willow to what I'd witnessed in Allcot's office. What she did with that information was entirely up to her. But I thought she should be aware of what kind of changes my presence in her life had caused. She'd either hate me forever or consider me her savior. It was a fair guess for either option.

I'd been sitting upstairs, gazing out the window at the large oak trees, when I heard the faint rumble of a familiar vehicle. The Trooper. I'd know it anywhere. Of course I hadn't seen a damned thing. I'd just heard it. That was when I'd gone running outside, frantically searching for something I'd never see.

And then there she was. My doppelgänger appeared out of nowhere, and with no conscious help from me, my feet carried me through the portal and right into Dax's arms.

"Dax!" I cried, tears streaming down my face.

He laughed and swung me around, burying his face in my neck. "Jesus, Phoebs. I thought I was never going to hold you again."

"I'm here," I said, my words both a confirmation and a promise. "I'm right here."

He pulled back slightly, staring down at me. "Are you all right?"

"I am now," I said and plastered myself to him again, never wanting to let go. I'd known I'd missed him, but I hadn't realized just how much until right at that moment.

"Okay, break it up," Seth said with a chuckle. "Let me see my sister for a minute before I cross back over."

His words hit me like a ton of bricks. There were things to say before he crossed. Reluctantly, I stepped away from Dax and turned to my brother. Behind him I spotted Leo, who was sitting in the front seat of the Trooper, watching us. I gave him a big wave, more than thrilled to see him. He waved back, but the motion was tentative as if he was unsure of his actions. I frowned. That wasn't like Leo.

"Hey, sis," Seth said, pulling me to him in a brotherly hug. "How are things back at the homestead?" He gestured to the plantation. "Anything I should know about before I walk into a firestorm?"

I bit down on my lip and nodded.

"Uh-oh. That doesn't sound good." His expression was strained as he watched me. It was about to get way worse.

"I'm not sure where to start." There was unmistakable guilt in my tone, and I mentally kicked myself. I was a badass investigator who regularly went undercover. Why couldn't I figure out how to lie to my brother?

"What happened?"

I took a deep breath and blurted, "Allcot knows everything."

Seth frowned. "What does that mean? Everything?"

"He knows about me not being his wife, about the portal, about you being from this world. Heather. He knows everything."

Seth shrugged. "Okay. That's not the end of the world. You made it back okay, so he must've taken it better than I thought."

I snorted out a humorless laugh. "You told me he'd likely kill me if he knew I wasn't 'his Phoebe.'"

"Well, okay. That might have been a slight exaggeration, but you just never know with that guy. I thought it was better to keep this to ourselves. It's fine, Phoebs. I'll handle it. I always do."

"He also knows about his counterpart here. He knows Allcot is a rich bastard who runs this city."

Seth actually chuckled at that. "It's not that different from what he is in that world."

"Yes, it is. And he made me tell him everything, Seth. All about Pandora and their relationship too."

Seth sucked in a sharp breath. "He knows he's supposed to be with Pandora?"

I winced again. "Yes."

"Fuck!" He started to move toward the area where the portal would be, but I grabbed his arm and pulled him back.

"There's more you have to know."

"What more could there possibly be?" he asked, clearly frustrated.

"I found him and Pandora together. They were… um… you know."

"Fucking?" he asked, almost dispassionately.

"Yeah, that." I studied him, taking in his furrowed brow and slight frown. He didn't look like a jealous husband. More like an annoyed brother. "You're not upset about that?"

He shrugged one shoulder. "I've been expecting it for years. Honestly, I guess I'm glad it's finally happened. Now we can stop pretending."

Well, that was a relief. "And Heather?" I asked, hopeful.

A little bit of light flashed in his eyes as he said, "It's possible, I guess. But that was a long time ago, and there's still Allcot to navigate." He reached out and caressed my cheek. "Listen, Phoebs, I know you're worried about me. But don't. I can handle myself. I've been doing it a long time. Now that you're back home where you belong, that's all that matters." He nodded to Dax, who was waiting for me by the Trooper. "He's a good man, and I gather a fucking good partner if he tracked you all the way to this place."

"He did?" I asked, astonished.

"He did," Seth said with a nod. "He was so close you probably heard the rumble of his engine."

That was entirely possible. I'd heard it today.

"Just do me a favor and hang on to each other, all right? Someone should get their happy ending."

I smiled up at him, feeling the burn of tears in my eyes. I didn't want him to go. But I knew he had to. Lex was on the other side, waiting for him. I'd even managed to find a way to look Allcot in the eye and tell him to forget about my demand to send Seth back to this world. He'd been so agreeable after his romp with Pandora, he'd just grinned and said, "Whatever you want, Phoebe."

Now I had to stand here and say goodbye to my brother forever. It fucking sucked. There was no holding the tears back any longer. I grabbed him, hugged him tight, and said, "I love you, Seth. Make sure Lex remembers me. Tell him every day how much I love him and miss him."

Seth kissed the top of my head. "I will, Phoebs. And one day, when you and that shifter of yours are ready, you'll bring a little one into this world and you'll be the best damned mother that ever lived."

I chuckled. "Don't go saddling me with kids just yet. Dax and I haven't even gotten to the 'will you go steady with me' phase yet."

A bark of laughter escaped from Seth and he snorted. "Oh, little sister, you are way past that stage. Trust me. That man is in love with you. Hook, line, and sinker."

I glanced back at Dax, squinting at him. "You think?"

"I don't think. I know."

His tone was so sure that I didn't bother debating him. I just grinned like a fool and said, "Thanks for telling me that. I love him too."

"Don't tell me. Tell him." He turned me around, kissed me once on the cheek, and then gently nudged me toward

Dax. Our eyes met and I felt all the tension from the past week drain right out of me.

"Take care of yourself, Seth," I said, glancing over my shoulder, but before I'd finished saying the words, my only brother disappeared into thin air. I stood rooted to the earth, staring at the spot where he'd just been. A tiny hole formed in my heart, and I knew it would forever be the place only Seth could fill.

"Hey," Dax said. "Ready to go home?"

I turned to look into his beautiful dark eyes and said, "When I'm with you, I'm already home."

It was sappy as fuck, but it made my heart flutter when he gave me that lopsided grin, making it more than worth it.

Chapter Twenty-Seven

"Just tell me one thing," Dax said. He was sitting on my bed, boots off, feet crossed at the ankle as he watched me rub lotion over my bare legs.

"What's that?" I asked from my spot in the doorway of my en suite bathroom where I'd just changed into the sexiest black lace bra and panty set.

"What did you think of the Dax in the parallel universe?"

I groaned. "You don't really want to talk about this right now, do you?"

A wolfish smile broke out over his handsome face. "I was just hoping to prolong the show for a little while longer."

"Right." I rolled my eyes. "Why don't you tell me what you thought of the faux Phoebe?"

"Honestly?"

"Yes," I said, my tone suddenly serious. "Did you like her better than me?"

"What? Hell no. She knocked me out and tied me up."

I raised one eyebrow. "I thought that was a fantasy of yours?"

"Sure, if it involves blow jobs and plenty of sex. That wasn't on the menu," he said dryly. "Besides, she wasn't you."

Uh-oh. Now was the time I had to come clean about the runaway kissing with the other Dax. "Listen—"

"What I mean is, she wasn't anything like you. The other Phoebe is jaded and vengeful. You're nothing like that. You care about the people around you, put your life on the line for them, but you're also soft and caring in a way that keeps you from being hardened. I think the other Phoebe has been through an awful lot that colors her perspective."

"You can say that again," I agreed. "Let's just say she's had a lot of tough knocks, and if she's kinda bitchy, I understand why."

"Okay, fair enough," he said, rising from the bed and pulling me to him. His hands slipped down to gently cup my ass just as his lips brushed over my jawline. "Now, what about my counterpart? What did you think?"

I smiled up at him. "You're wonderful in both worlds."

His eyes glittered with amusement. "Really? Was he this wonderful?" Dax dipped his head and trailed hot kisses over my bare shoulder.

"No." I laughed and tilted my head, giving him better access. "Not nearly that wonderful."

"That's good. I'd hate to have to kick my own ass for touching my woman."

I pulled back slightly and pressed a hand to his chest. "There is something I need to tell you. Actually a couple of somethings before we go any further tonight."

His muscles tensed as all his amusement fled. "Do I need to be sitting down for this?"

"Probably not. It's not that serious." I gave him a tentative smile. "But in the interest of full disclosure... You should know that the other Dax did kiss me. A couple of times."

"Why?" he asked, sounding more curious than angry.

"Because he's in love with the other Phoebe, and they haven't been together in years."

"But she's married to Allcot, right?"

I nodded. "Yeah, but I was helping him out of a really shitty situation, and he kinda thought it was her. Emotions were running high. I don't know. Mine were too. He was… like you. We were a team and everything sucked. I just… I missed you, Dax. I wanted comfort from you, and he…" I clamped my mouth shut, realizing I was rambling. "I'm sorry. It's not an excuse. But I thought you should know. I'm not a cheater. This was just a really strange thing and—"

"Forget it," he said, his voice husky with emotion. "I understand."

"You do?"

"Of course I do, Phoebs." He brushed a lock of hair off my shoulder, letting his fingers trail over to my neck.

The movement made me flinch, and I hated myself for it.

"Whoa," he said gently. "What was that?"

I squeezed my eyes shut, wanting to forget the memory. But I knew I had to tell him. I couldn't let Allcot's bullshit come between us. "You know that while I was there, I stayed at Allcot's, right?"

"Yeah." His hand came up and cupped my cheek. "It's okay, Phoebe. You can tell me."

"Well, he did that. Ran his hands over my neck, brushed his fingers over my pulse, and then…" I hesitated, not wanting to say the words.

"And then?" he prompted gently.

"Fuck." My eyes flew open, and I knew they were blazing with red-hot anger. "That fucking bastard bit me."

"He bit you?" Dax repeated as if he hadn't heard me the first time. "As in sank his fangs into your neck and drank from you?" The anger in his shaking tone matched mine, and I knew I had to rein it in or he was likely to lose his shit, just like I was every time I thought about it.

"Yeah. But I stopped it. It only happened once." Though he'd acted like he'd do it again.

"How?"

"I kicked him in the balls." It wasn't completely true, but I'd intended to, and that was enough.

Dax was silent as he stared at me, then he threw his head back and laughed. "Of course you did. Damn, that's my girl."

His levity was exactly what I needed, and I slipped one knee over his thighs to straddle him.

"You're not mad?" I asked, taking his face in my hands.

"At you? No. Should I be?"

I shook my head. "You're the only one I want sharing my bed."

"That's a damned good thing, Phoebe Kilsen, because if anyone else tries to climb into it, shit is going to go down."

"You're pretty cocky for a guy who hasn't even asked me to be his girlfriend," I said, my tone light and teasing, but there was much more behind those words. After my ordeal, I felt the need to define what we were to each other. I knew how I felt and was ready to tell him. But I had to be sure it was the right time.

"You don't know if you're my girlfriend or not?" he asked, surprise in his tone. "Seriously?"

"We've never talked about it."

An impatient noise sounded deep in this throat. "Phoebs, I've gone way past the girlfriend-boyfriend label. I don't know about you, but I'm just about ready to move right into this bedroom and never leave."

I felt a smile claim my lips. "Yeah? What if Willow and Tal aren't interested in a fourth roommate?"

"Then you better get packing, 'cause you're moving into my place."

I started to say something about his cramped apartment, but he cut me off with a kiss. His lips were hot. Urgent. Hungry. And so were mine. I'd wanted him the moment we'd stepped through the door. But I'd had to hug Willow and Tal and give them a basic rundown of my ordeal.

It hadn't taken Dax long to get impatient and tug me into my room though. He'd made an excuse about my needing my rest, but we both knew that wasn't going to happen. We needed each other. Needed that connection that made us feel alive and loved and real.

"Come closer, Phoebs," Dax ordered, pulling me up so that I was straddling his lap, my breasts pressing into his bare chest.

He was rock-hard male everywhere. And I do mean everywhere. The bulge in his boxers was already pushing against the strip of the black lace between my legs, and I wanted him. Needed him to fill me, claim me, make me his again.

"Kiss me, Dax," I ordered. "Make my head spin so hard all I know is you and your touch."

"You got it, sweetheart." But instead of capturing my lips, he dipped his head and pressed his lips to the swell of my breast. His soft lips were glorious on my already heated skin. One hand came up to cup my other breast, his fingers gently tracing the edge of the lace. It felt wondrous. Every touch, every caress, every little kiss ratcheted up my need, making me so I was already writhing against him, and we hadn't even gotten out of our clothes yet.

"Dax," I said breathily.

"Yeah, love?" His fingers found one of my nipples and lightly pinched the sensitive peak.

"Oh, that's good." I bent my head and caught his lips in a kiss that was so hot I felt as if I were going to combust right there, with layers of fabric between us, before he'd ever even touched me.

"Jesus, Phoebe," he said with a moan when he broke away. "I need to lose these boxers."

"Let me," I said, grinning up at him as I shimmied down his body, taking the boxers with me. And then I slowly made my way back up, my hands gliding along his inner thighs until I wrapped one hand around his glorious erection.

"God," he said, closing his eyes, his hips jerking forward slightly as I stroked him.

"You're beautiful, Dax," I said and leaned over him, running my tongue over the tip of his cock.

"Jesus," he said on a groan, and I started to wonder if I tortured him long enough if he'd run through the entire list of deities. But I'd have to find out another day, because suddenly Dax reached down, pulled me up, and rolled. His lips crashed down on mine, his hands everywhere.

Before I knew it, he had my pretty bra and panties on the floor, leaving us both completely naked. He paused for a moment, lifted himself up so he was hovering over me, and just gazed down at my body.

I smiled up at him. "Now what's your plan?"

"Everything," he said with a growl and dropped kisses on

my breasts, my stomach, my hips, my thighs, and then he ran those big strong hands up my inner thighs, spreading me for him before he dove into me, his mouth teasing, tasting, taking everything I had to offer.

I buried my hands in his thick hair and held on as he laved my clit, working it so thoroughly and with such expertise that it seemed like only a second passed before I was clenching around him and crying out his name.

"That's my girl," he said huskily as he worked his way back up my body, taking his time to plant more kisses and tease my nipples until I was moaning again.

"Dax," I panted. "Please."

His dark eyes bored into mine as he reached down, palming himself. "Is this what you need, love?"

I glanced down and nearly came at the sight of him holding himself. "God, yes. That's exactly what I need."

"All right, love. It's all yours." But instead of entering me like I wanted him to, he placed his tip against my already sensitive flesh and stroked me until he was once again teasing my clit.

"Oh fuck, Dax. It's too much. Too sensitive. Too— Oh!" I cried out, coming again with an intensity I'd never experienced before. My body shuddered beneath him, the wave taking me right over the edge. But he didn't give me time to fade away on that ride, because he was already pushing into me with a groan of pleasure that brought me right back to reality.

"There," I said. "Right there. Perfect."

He was buried inside me, holding himself there, waiting for me to get used to him. But there was no need to wait. I was ready and pumped my hips, demanding more.

He didn't disappoint. Dax stared down at me, his

movements slow and deliberate. Everything tingled, and as we locked gazes, everything else in the world fell away, and all I knew was this man. The one I knew without a doubt would cross universes to find me if he had to. Love rolled off him, filling me up from head to toe.

It didn't take long before the ache started from deep inside me and I started to demand more. Harder, faster, deeper. Dax obliged all my demands, never taking his gaze from mine, even watching me as my breath quickened, and my body tensed, and then I shattered. Through it all, he was there, giving me what I needed, witnessing it all, until I finally stilled and smiled up at him.

"Did you get what you needed, gorgeous?" he asked, his eyes still sparkling with lust.

"Yes," I said. "Definitely."

"Good. My turn." He raised my hands over my head and held them there as he thrust into me in hard, long strokes, loving me with every inch of him until both of us were breathing hard and moaning with pleasure. "Are you going to come one last time for me, love?" he gasped out.

The sound of his rough, needy voice was all I needed. My muscles started to clench around him, and he buried himself in me one last time before we both shattered.

I WOKE deep in the night to find Dax propped up on one arm, just watching me. I blinked a couple of times and smiled up at him. "You know that's a little creepy, right?"

He chuckled. "Maybe a little. You just looked so gorgeous lying there naked in the moonlight."

I glanced at the window, noting the large full moon

shining its light across the bed, illuminating me. Chuckling, I placed his free hand on one of my breasts just to feel the weight of him there. "I think I can give you a pass then."

"Good." He dipped his head and placed a kiss on my cheek even as I rolled onto my side, curling up next to him. We lay there silently for a few beats, then he said, "I love you, Phoebe. Do you know that?"

The words filtered over me, warming me all the way to my toes. A tiny smile claimed my lips when I said, "Yes, I did." I twisted my head so that I could see his face when I added, "I love you too, handsome."

"Of course you do," he said with a tiny chuckle. "Now go back to sleep. I have a big morning planned."

"Oh? Is it more bedroom Olympics?"

He pressed his lips to my shoulder and said, "Something like that."

Chapter Twenty-Eight

"*I* think this is just about perfect," I said, eyeing the giant twelve-foot Christmas tree. "What about you, Wil?"

My friend placed her hands on her growing belly and said, "Looks good to me. How are we going to get it back to the house?"

"They have delivery," Talisen said, coming up behind her and wrapping his arms around her waist.

"My god. Could you two get any more nauseating?" I grinned. The truth was, they were gorgeous. Willow was five months pregnant and glowing so brightly I almost needed sunglasses to look at her. And Talisen, he was bubbling over with joy. I wasn't quite sure how his coworkers dealt with him on a daily basis. I'd had to escape to Dax's on a regular basis just to avoid a permanent toothache.

"I've found it," Dax said, a huge grin on his face.

"Oh?" I chuckled, already knowing it was going to be something ridiculous. Dax had already picked out a dead tree, a two footer that was decorated with condoms, and a light-up naked Santa. At this rate, we were going end up decorating with strings of popcorn and calling it done.

"It's right over here," he said, pulling me through the Christmas tree lot.

The day was cool and slightly drizzly, but the weather didn't dampen my mood at all. Dax and I had the next few days off and were spending it moving into our new house. After Willow and Talisen had found out they were pregnant, we'd decided it was time to find our own place. Of course it had ended up being just three doors down from Willow and Tal, but in my eyes that made it perfect. I'd be right there, ready and willing to help with everything baby without being under their feet. To say I was excited about being an auntie was an understatement.

"This one," Dax said, pointing to the biggest tree I'd ever seen.

I laughed. "Seriously, Dax? Where are we going to put that? We have a twelve-foot ceiling, not a vaulted entry."

He rolled his eyes. "You didn't even look at it carefully."

"Yes I did, I—" Just as I was saying the words, I saw a very familiar head poke out from behind the mammoth tree. "Seth?" I cried out, my voice going high like a five-year-old's.

His low chuckle rumbled from behind the tree, and I screeched again. "Seth!"

Without waiting for anyone to respond, I darted around the tree just in time to see him snatch a little boy into his arms and tilt his head in, whispering something.

"Lex!" I practically screamed as I darted toward them, nearly knocking them over with the biggest hug that ever existed. "Oh my god! How? What? When did you get here? How long can you stay? Tell me everything. I'm dying to know what's going on back… um, home?"

"Hi, little sis," Seth said with a huge smile and handed Lex to me. "Someone has been dying to give you a hug of his own."

I hefted the child into my arms, nearly crumpling under his weight. This one was all boy.

"Auntie Phoebe," he said, his face all smiles and joy, just the way I remembered my brother as a young boy.

"Hey, sweetheart," I said, nuzzling his nose. "I missed you so much. Have you been reading?"

He nodded. "Heather reads to me every night."

My head jerked up as I stared right at Seth. "Heather?" I echoed, putting him on the spot right there in the Christmas tree lot.

"Present," a giggling voice said from behind me. I whirled around and spotted the raven-haired girl I'd known so many years ago. Her eyes were just as green and her golden skin just as lovely. But there was a maturity to her now that hadn't been there before. She seemed more confident, content. Though I supposed we all did compared to when we were teenagers.

"Heather," I said, my voice soft and full of affection. "I'm so glad to see you."

"Mama," Lex said, reaching for Heather.

She took one of his hands in hers but made no move to take him from me. "Your Auntie Phoebe has you right now, sweetie. I'll hold you a little later."

He bobbed his head toward her, his sweet smile turning hearts to mush everywhere. But Heather was not swayed. She reached out and took Seth's hand in her free one and tugged him closer, as if she was taking advantage of the child-free moment.

I just beamed at them. "I can't believe you're here."

"I'm glad you seem happy because I have some bad news for you, sis," Seth said, his eyes flashing with amusement.

"What?" I asked suspiciously. "Something's going on, and I'm so happy to see you right now that I don't even care, but someone's going to have to tell me sooner or later."

"Yeah, there's definitely something going on," Dax said, finally finding his way to my side. "Remember those two spare offices we thought we were going to have in the house?"

I cut my gaze from Dax to Seth and back again, trying to keep my excitement in check. "Yeah. What about them?"

"Looks like we're going to need to keep using the kitchen table a little longer, because we're about to have permanent houseguests."

I closed my eyes and chanted, "Please don't let this be a dream. Please don't let this be a dream." On my third chant, I felt a small hand land on my cheek. I opened my eyes and stared into the sweet face of my nephew Lex.

"It's not a dream, Auntie," he said sweetly. "It can't be, because if it is, I'm having the exact same dream."

My laughter was instantaneous. "You're right, baby. It can't be a dream. You wanna go home and get settled in? Maybe a cup of hot chocolate?"

"Hot chocolate," he started to chant over and over again in much the same way I'd just been doing.

"Perfect," Seth said with a chuckle. "Maybe he'll wear himself out doing that instead of running around the house."

"Don't count on it," Heather said with a chuckle.

I eyed them, my curiosity about the situation flying off the charts. But instead of asking them what was up, I turned to Dax. "We still need a tree. You're in charge. Get a good one. One that fits!"

He saluted me. "Yes, ma'am. See you at home."

I beckoned my brother and Heather. "Ready to see the new digs?"

"More than ready. It's been one hell of a week."

I grinned at them. "Where have I heard that before?"

Seth laughed. "It's really good to see you, Phoebs."

"You too, brother. Now follow me to the car. I have lots of questions."

Seth and Heather shared a glance, and I couldn't help but wonder what kind of secrets were lurking under there. But then maybe not. After my visit to another parallel universe, I could honestly say it wasn't something I ever wanted to do again.

"Seth?" I asked as we reached my Charger.

"Yeah?"

"Just tell me one thing. Is this just a visit or a permanent change?"

He reached out and squeezed my hand. "Permanent."

My heart swelled, and I thought it might burst right out of my chest. "Good."

I TRIED to keep my questions in check until everyone was settled around the table. It was the one piece of furniture we'd managed to move in. The rest of the house was empty, much to Lex's delight as he ran around, making his cries echo off the plaster walls. We'd only moved in a week ago, and most of our furniture was on order. Dax had left his at his old place, where Leo was taking over the lease. Now that Leo had graduated from his training and was a full-fledged Void agent, he was more than ready to live on his own. Though, I had been a little disappointed when he'd turned down my invitation to live at our place. I kinda liked having him around.

Turning my attention to my brother, I said, "Okay. I can't stand it. What happened? How did you end up back here?"

Again the pair shared a look, this one wistful.

"You guys are killing me. Details, now!"

Seth sat back in his chair and draped an arm over the empty seat next to him. "I think we might owe you a thank-you."

"Me? Why?"

"Because without that deal you made with Allcot, we might not be here today."

"What deal?" I asked stupidly. "I haven't seen Allcot in months actually."

"I don't mean the one from this world," he said easily. "I mean the one you saw banging Pandora on his desk six months ago."

That made me sit up straight. "My deal? The one to set Willow and Dax free?"

"That and the one to send us home," Seth said with a one-armed shrug.

"No. No!" I pressed my hand to my forehead, fighting the headache again. "I told him to call off that part. I didn't want to be making decisions for your lives that weren't my decisions to make."

"Hmm, well it seems you did, and you did us a huge favor. You see, it took six months for the witches Allcot hired to figure out how to reseal a couple of the portals. There were two that kept giving them trouble. And by then the other Phoebe had left to find Dax, and Pandora and I were already divorced. Her actions during her honeymoon period with Allcot led to some… interesting developments, and long story short, I ended up with custody of Lex."

I glanced over at my nephew and smiled at him as he rolled a toy truck over the old hardwood. "Custody. Wow. I wouldn't have thought that was an option considering how powerful Allcot is."

"You and me both, Phoebs," he said and shook his head as if he still didn't believe it. "Anyway, when it came time to close the portals, they couldn't do it until all the other spells were stripped. One of them was yours."

"Wait. I didn't bind that spell." I stared at them in confusion.

"You didn't, but Allcot did using your DNA. He hired Genevieve to do it for him, and all he needed was a piece of your hair or a used toothbrush. Since you were living there, it was easy for her to get."

"Anyway, she cast the original one and it took her some time to figure out how to strip it. Once that was done, the city wanted to close the portals, and that meant we had to go."

"And Lex? How did Pandora take it?"

Seth glanced over at his son. "She's not really in his life much anymore."

"She's a new vampire," Heather said. "All she wants is blood and sex. It's not conducive to raising a child."

"Oh my god," I gasped out. "That's what you mean by her actions during her honeymoon period?"

Seth nodded, his expression turning angry. But as soon as he looked at Heather, she placed a soothing hand over his and smiled. His anger vanished, replaced by something that looked a lot like contentment.

My heart was so full I thought it might burst. "You guys," I said, fighting back tears. "I'm so glad you're here."

"We are too," Heather said. "And we promise not to impose for too long. We just need a bit of a buffer to get situated in this reality."

"Please don't worry about it. Stay as long as you like. Heck, stay forever."

"That's right," Dax said as he walked through the door, wrestling a large tree that looked maybe a little overkill for the space, but I just looked around and grinned. A new house, Dax, and Seth's family, with Willow and Talisen just a few doors down.

My life was just about perfect. Now all I needed was a new dagger to replace the one I'd broken off in the chest of a vamp last week.

"Phoebs, come here. I have something for you," Dax said.

"Again? What's next, a puppy?" I made my way back to the den where we were going to keep the tree.

"I doubt it's a puppy. Not unless it's a really flat one." Dax was standing next to the undecorated tree, holding a box. He held it out for me. "It's for you."

"Why?" I asked suspiciously.

"Because Santa dropped it off as a housewarming gift, that's why." Dax kissed my forehead and whispered, "Hurry up. We're all dying to see what it is."

"Right." Judging by the uneven wrapping job with two different types of paper, I was guessing Dax had done it himself. But I didn't care. I was just excited to get another present. Once I ripped the paper off, I stared down at the embossed box lid.

DAGGERS & DIAMONDS was scrolled across the front.

"Oh! Diamonds?" Heather asked, her interest piqued.

Seth laughed. "Not if he knows what's good for him.

Phoebe isn't exactly a jewelry girl unless it's vintage jewelry or silver."

"Daggers then?" Heather whispered, and I saw the woman open her mouth in shock as if women didn't have a weapons collection.

"God, I hope so," I said and ripped the lid off. I stared down at the gorgeous rose-gold hilt with a gleaming silver blade, taking in the intricate design that crept like vines up the hilt. "Oh, Dax. It's gorgeous," I gushed. "I can't believe you did this."

"Why wouldn't I? Only the best for my girl, right?" Dax pulled me into a hug while I fought to hold back tears.

He glanced down at me. "Tears for the dagger but not for your brother moving here permanently?"

I huffed out a laugh. "That dagger is a total piece of art."

"So are you, Phoebs," he said. "So are you."

Deanna's Book List

Pyper Rayne Novels:
Spirits, Stilettos, and a Silver Bustier
Spirits, Rock Stars, and a Midnight Chocolate Bar
Spirits, Beignets, and a Bayou Biker Gang
Spirits, Diamonds, and a Drive-thru Daiquiri Stand
Spirits, Spells, and Wedding Bells

Jade Calhoun Novels:
Haunted on Bourbon Street
Witches of Bourbon Street
Demons of Bourbon Street
Angels of Bourbon Street
Shadows of Bourbon Street
Incubus of Bourbon Street
Bewitched on Bourbon Street
Hexed on Bourbon Street
Dragons of Bourbon Street

Witches of Keating Hollow:

Soul of the Witch
Heart of the Witch
Spirit of the Witch
Dreams of the Witch
Courage of the Witch
Love of the Witch

Last Witch Standing:

Soulless at Sunset
Bloodlust By Midnight
Bitten At Daybreak

Witch Island Brides:

The Vampire's Last Dance
The Wolf's New Year Bride
The Warlock's Enchanted Kiss
The Shifter's First Bite

Crescent City Fae Novels:

Influential Magic
Irresistible Magic
Intoxicating Magic

Destiny Novels:

Defining Destiny
Accepting Fate

About the Author

New York Times and USA Today bestselling author, Deanna Chase, is a native Californian, transplanted to the slower paced lifestyle of southeastern Louisiana. When she isn't writing, she is often goofing off with her husband in New Orleans or playing with her two shih tzu dogs. For more information and updates on newest releases visit her website at deannachase.com.